John Griffith London (born **John Griffith Chaney**; January 12, 1876 – November 22, 1916) was an American novelist, journalist, and social activist. A pioneer in the world of commercial magazine fiction, he was one of the first writers to become a worldwide celebrity and earn a large fortune from writing. He was also an innovator in the genre that would later become known as science fiction. His most famous works include The Call of the Wild and White Fang, both set in the Klondike Gold Rush, as well as the short stories "To Build a Fire", "An Odyssey of the North", and "Love of Life". He also wrote about the South Pacific in stories such as "The Pearls of Parlay" and "The Heathen". London was part of the radical literary group "The Crowd" in San Francisco and a passionate advocate of unionization, socialism, and the rights of workers. He wrote several powerful works dealing with these topics, such as his dystopian novel The Iron Heel, his non-fiction exposé The People of the Abyss, and The War of the Classes. (Source: Wikipedia)

Literary works:
The Cruise of the Dazzler (1902)
A Daughter of the Snows (1902)
The Call of the Wild (1903)
The Kempton-Wace Letters (1903)
The Sea-Wolf (1904)
The Game (1905)
White Fang (1906)
Before Adam (1907)
The Iron Heel (1908)
Martin Eden (1909)
Burning Daylight (1910)
Adventure (1911)
The Scarlet Plague (1912)
A Son of the Sun (1912)
The Abysmal Brute (1913)
The Valley of the Moon (1913)

THE ACORN-PLANTER
A CALIFORNIA FOREST PLAY
&
STORIES OF SHIPS
AND THE SEA LITTLE BLUE BOOK #1169

JACK LONDON

PRINCE CLASSICS

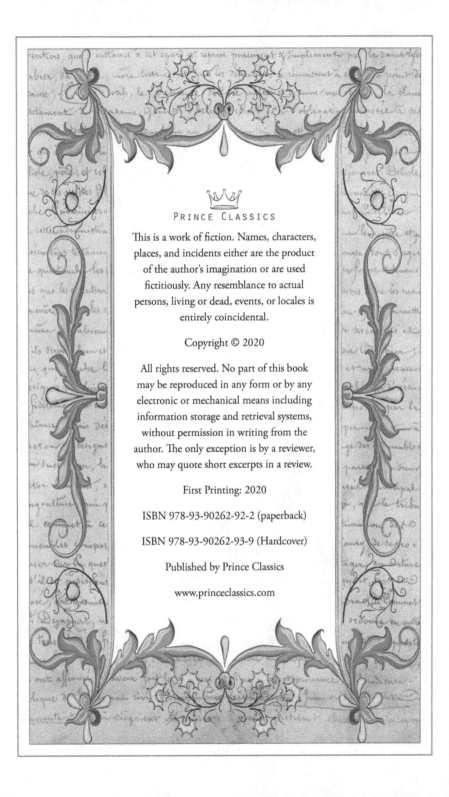

PRINCE CLASSICS

First Printing: 2020

ISBN 978-93-90262-92-2 (paperback)

ISBN 978-93-90262-93-9 (Hardcover)

Published by Prince Classics

www.princeclassics.com

Contents

THE ACORN-PLANTER
A CALIFORNIA FOREST PLAY

&

STORIES OF SHIPS
AND THE SEA LITTLE BLUE BOOK #1169

THE ACORN-PLANTER: A
CALIFORNIA FOREST PLAY

ARGUMENT

In the morning of the world, while his tribe
makes its camp for the night in a grove, Red
Cloud, the first man of men, and the first man
of the Nishinam, save in war, sings of the duty
of life, which duty is to make life more abundant.
The Shaman, or medicine man, sings of
foreboding and prophecy. The War Chief, who
commands in war, sings that war is the only
way to life. This Red Cloud denies, affirming
that the way of life is the way of the acorn-
planter, and that whoso slays one man slays
the planter of many acorns. Red Cloud wins
the Shaman and the people to his contention.
After the passage of thousands of years, again
in the grove appear the Nishinam. In Red
Cloud, the War Chief, the Shaman, and the
Dew-Woman are repeated the eternal figures
of the philosopher, the soldier, the priest, and
the woman—types ever realizing themselves
afresh in the social adventures of man. Red
Cloud recognizes the wrecked explorers as

planters and life-makers, and is for treating

them with kindness. But the War Chief and

the idea of war are dominant The Shaman

joins with the war party, and is privy to the

massacre of the explorers.

A hundred years pass, when, on their seasonal

migration, the Nishinam camp for the night in

the grove. They still live, and the war formula

for life seems vindicated, despite the imminence

of the superior life-makers, the whites, who are

flooding into California from north, south, east,

and west—the English, the Americans, the

Spaniards, and the Russians. The massacre by

the white men follows, and Red Cloud, dying,

recognizes the white men as brother acorn-planters,

the possessors of the superior life-formula

of which he had always been a protagonist.

In the Epilogue, or Apotheosis, occur the

celebration of the death of war and the triumph

of the acorn-planters.

PROLOGUE

Time. In the morning of the world.

Scene. A forest hillside where great trees stand with wide spaces between. A stream flows from a spring that bursts out of the hillside. It is a place of lush ferns and brakes, also, of thickets of such shrubs as inhabit a redwood forest floor. At the left, in the open level space at the foot of the hillside, extending out of sight among the trees, is visible a portion of a Nishinam Indian camp. It is a temporary camp for the night. Small cooking fires smoulder. Standing about are withe-woven baskets for the carrying of supplies and dunnage. Spears and bows and quivers of arrows lie about. Boys drag in dry branches for firewood. Young women fill gourds with water from the stream and proceed about their camp tasks. A number of older women are pounding acorns in stone mortars with stone pestles. An old man and a Shaman, or priest, look expectantly up the hillside. All wear moccasins and are skin-clad, primitive, in their garmenting. Neither iron nor woven cloth occurs in the weapons and gear.

ACT I.

Shaman

(Looking up hillside.)

Red Cloud is late.

Old Man

(After inspection of hillside.)

He has chased the deer far. He is patient.

In the chase he is patient like an old man.

Shaman

His feet are as fleet as the deer's.

Old Man

(Nodding.)

And he is more patient than the deer.

Shaman

(Assertively, as if inculcating a lesson.)

He is a mighty chief.

Old Man

(Nodding.)

His father was a mighty chief. He is like to

his father.

Shaman

(More assertively.)

He is his father. It is so spoken. He is
his father's father. He is the first man, the
first Red Cloud, ever born, and born again, to
chiefship of his people.

Old Man

It is so spoken.

Shaman

His father was the Coyote. His mother was
the Moon. And he was the first man.

Old Man

(Repeating.)

His father was the Coyote. His mother was
the Moon. And he was the first man.

Shaman

He planted the first acorns, and he is very
wise.

Old Man

(Repeating.)

He planted the first acorns, and he is very
wise.

(Cries from the women and a turning of
faces. Red Cloud appears among his
hunters descending the hillside. All

carry spears, and bows and arrows.

Some carry rabbits and other small

game. Several carry deer)

PLAINT OF THE NISHINAM

Red Cloud, the meat-bringer!

Red Cloud, the acorn-planter!

Red Cloud, first man of the Nishinam!

Thy people hunger.

Far have they fared.

Hard has the way been.

Day long they sought,

High in the mountains,

Deep in the pools,

Wide 'mong the grasses,

In the bushes, and tree-tops,

Under the earth and flat stones.

Few are the acorns,

Past is the time for berries,

Fled are the fishes, the prawns and the grasshoppers,

Blown far are the grass-seeds,

Flown far are the young birds,

Old are the roots and withered.

Built are the fires for the meat.

Laid are the boughs for sleep,

Yet thy people cannot sleep.

Red Cloud, thy people hunger.

Red Cloud

(Still descending.)

Good hunting! Good hunting!

Hunters

Good hunting! Good hunting!

(Completing the descent, Red Cloud

motions to the meat-bearers. They throw

down their burdens before the women,

who greedily inspect the spoils.)

MEAT SONG OF THE NISHINAM

Meat that is good to eat,

Tender for old teeth,

Gristle for young teeth,

Big deer and fat deer,

Lean meat and fat meat,

Haunch-meat and knuckle-bone,

Liver and heart.

Food for the old men,

Life for all men,

For women and babes.

Easement of hunger-pangs,

Sorrow destroying,

Laughter provoking,

Joy invoking,

In the smell of its smoking

And its sweet in the mouth.

(The younger women take charge of the meat,

and the older women resume their acorn-pounding.)

(Red Cloud approaches the acorn-pounders

and watches them with pleasure.

All group about him, the Shaman to the

fore, and hang upon his every action, his

every utterance.)

Red Cloud

The heart of the acorn is good?

First Old Woman

(Nodding.)

It is good food.

Red Cloud

When you have pounded and winnowed and

washed away the bitter.

Second Old Woman

As thou taught'st us, Red Cloud, when the

world was very young and thou wast the first man.

Red Cloud

It is a fat food. It makes life, and life is good.

Shaman

It was thou, Red Cloud, gathering the acorns

and teaching the storing, who gavest life to the

Nishinam in the lean years aforetime, when the

tribes not of the Nishinam passed like the dew

of the morning.

(He nods a signal to the Old Man.)

Old Man

In the famine in the old time,

When the old man was a young man,

When the heavens ceased from raining,

When the grasslands parched and withered,

When the fishes left the river,

And the wild meat died of sickness,

In the tribes that knew not acorns,

All their women went dry-breasted,

All their younglings chewed the deer-hides,

All their old men sighed and perished,

And the young men died beside them,

Till they died by tribe and totem,

And o'er all was death upon them.

Yet the Nishinam unvanquished,

Did not perish by the famine.

Oh, the acorns Red Cloud gave them!

Oh, the acorns Red Cloud taught them

How to store in willow baskets

'Gainst the time and need of famine!

Shaman

(Who, throughout the Old Man's recital, has

nodded approbation, turning to Red

Cloud.)

Sing to thy people, Red Cloud, the song of

life which is the song of the acorn.

Red Cloud

(Making ready to begin)

And which is the song of woman, O Shaman.

Shaman

(Hushing the people to listen, solemnly)

He sings with his father's lips, and with the

lips of his father's fathers to the beginning of time

and men.

SONG OF THE FIRST MAN

Red Cloud

I am Red Cloud,

The first man of the Nishinam.

My father was the Coyote.

My mother was the Moon.

The Coyote danced with the stars,

And wedded the Moon on a mid-summer night

The Coyote is very wise,

The Moon is very old,

Mine is his wisdom,

Mine is her age.

I am the first man.

I am the life-maker and the father of life.

I am the fire-bringer.

The Nishinam were the first men,

And they were without fire,

And knew the bite of the frost of bitter nights.

The panther stole the fire from the East,

The fox stole the fire from the panther,

The ground squirrel stole the fire from the fox,

And I, Red Cloud, stole the fire from the ground squirrel.

I, Red Cloud, stole the fire for the Nishinam,

And hid it in the heart of the wood.

To this day is the fire there in the heart of the wood.

I am the Acorn-Planter.

I brought down the acorns from heaven.

I planted the short acorns in the valley.

I planted the long acorns in the valley.

I planted the black-oak acorns that sprout, that sprout!

I planted the sho-kum and all the roots of the ground.

I planted the oat and the barley, the beaver-tail grass-nut,

The tar-weed and crow-foot, rock lettuce and ground lettuce,

And I taught the virtue of clover in the season of blossom,

The yellow-flowered clover, ball-rolled in its yellow dust.

I taught the cooking in baskets by hot stones from the fire,

Took the bite from the buckeye and soap-root

By ground-roasting and washing in the sweetness of water,

And of the manzanita the berry I made into flour,

Taught the way of its cooking with hot stones in sand pools,

And the way of its eating with the knobbed tail of the deer.

Taught I likewise the gathering and storing,

The parching and pounding

Of the seeds from the grasses and grass-roots;

And taught I the planting of seeds in the Nishinam home-camps,

In the Nishinam hills and their valleys,

In the due times and seasons,

To sprout in the spring rains and grow ripe in the sun.

Shaman

Hail, Red Cloud, the first man!

The People

Hail, Red Cloud, the first man!

Shaman

Who showedst us the way of our feet in the world!

The People

Who showedst us the way of our feet in the world!

Shaman

Who showedst us the way of our food in the world!

The People

Who showedst us the way of our food in the world!

Shaman

Who showedst us the way of our hearts in the world!

The People

Who showedst us the way of our hearts in the world!

Shaman

Who gavest us the law of family!

The People

Who gavest us the law of family!

Shaman

The law of tribe!

The People

The law of tribe!

Shaman

The law of totem!

The People

The law of totem!

Shaman

And madest us strong in the world among men!

The People

And madest us strong in the world among men!

Red Cloud

Life is good, O Shaman, and I have sung but half its song. Acorns are good. So is woman good. Strength is good. Beauty is good. So is kindness good. Yet are all these things without power except for woman. And by these things woman makes strong men, and strong men make for life, ever for more life.

War Chief

(With gesture of interruption that causes remonstrance from the Shaman but which Red Cloud acknowledges.)

I care not for beauty. I desire strength in battle and wind in the chase that I may kill my enemy and run down my meat.

Red Cloud

Well spoken, O War Chief. By voices in
council we learn our minds, and that, too, is
strength. Also, is it kindness. For kindness
and strength and beauty are one. The eagle in
the high blue of the sky is beautiful. The salmon
leaping the white water in the sunlight is beautiful.
The young man fastest of foot in the race
is beautiful. And because they fly well, and leap
well, and run well, are they beautiful. Beauty
must beget beauty. The ring-tail cat begets
the ring-tail cat, the dove the dove. Never
does the dove beget the ring-tail cat. Hearts
must be kind. The little turtle is not kind.
That is why it is the little turtle. It lays its
eggs in the sun-warm sand and forgets its young
forever. And the little turtle is forever the
Kttle turtle. But we are not little turtles,
because we are kind. We do not leave our young
to the sun in the sand. Our women keep our
young warm under their hearts, and, after, they
keep them warm with deer-skin and campfire.

Because we are kind we are men and not little

turtles, and that is why we eat the little turtle

that is not strong because it is not kind.

War Chief

(Gesturing to be heard.)

The Modoc come against us in their strength.

Often the Modoc come against us. We cannot

be kind to the Modoc.

Red Cloud

That will come after. Kindness grows. First

must we be kind to our own. After, long after,

all men will be kind to all men, and all men will

be very strong. The strength of the Nishinam

is not the strength of its strongest fighter. It is

the strength of all the Nishinam added together

that makes the Nishinam strong. We talk, you

and I, War Chief and First Man, because we are

kind one to the other, and thus we add together

our wisdom, and all the Nishinam are stronger

because we have talked.

(A voice is heard singing. Red Cloud

holds up his hand for silence.)

MATING SONG

Dew-Woman

In the morning by the river,

   In the evening at the fire,

In the night when all lay sleeping,

   Torn was I with life's desire.

There were stirrings 'neath my heart-beats

   Of the dreams that came to me;

In my ears were whispers, voices,

   Of the children yet to be.

Red Cloud

(As Red Cloud sings, Dew-Woman

steals from behind a tree and approaches

him.)

In the morning by the river

   Saw I first my maid of dew,

Daughter of the dew and dawnlight,

   Of the dawn and honey-dew.

She was laughter, she was sunlight,

   Woman, maid, and mate, and wife;

She was sparkle, she was gladness,

   She was all the song of life.

Dew-Woman

In the night I built my fire,

Fire that maidens foster when

In the ripe of mating season

 Each builds for her man of men.

Red Cloud

In the night I sought her, proved her,

 Found her ease, content, and rest,

After day of toil and struggle

 Man's reward on woman's breast.

Dew-Woman

Came to me my mate and lover;

 Kind the hands he laid on me;

Wooed me gently as a man may,

 Father of the race to be.

Red Cloud

Soft her arms about me bound me,

 First man of the Nishinam,

Arms as soft as dew and dawnlight,

 Daughter of the Nishinam.

Red Cloud

She was life and she was woman!

Dew-Woman

He was life and he was man!

Red Cloud and Dew-Woman

(Arms about each other.)

In the dusk-time of our love-night,

   There beside the marriage fire,

Proved we all the sweets of living,

   In the arms of our desire.

War Chief

(Angrily.)

The councils of men are not the place for
women.

Red Cloud

(Gently.)

As men grow kind and wise there will be
women in the councils of men. As men grow
their women must grow with them if they would
continue to be the mothers of men.

War Chief

It is told of old time that there are women in
the councils of the Sim. And is it not told that
the Sun Man will destroy us?

Red Cloud

Then is the Sun Man the stronger; it may be
because of his kindness and wiseness, and because
of his women.

Young Brave

Is it told that the women of the Sun are good

to the eye, soft to the arm, and a fire in the heart

of man?

Shaman

(Holding up hand solemnly.)

It were well, lest the young do not forget, to

repeat the old word again.

War Chief

(Nodding confirmation.)

Here, where the tale is told.

(Pointing to the spring.)

Here, where the water burst from under the heel

of the Sun Man mounting into the sky.

(War Chief leads the way up the hillside

to the spring, and signals to the Old Man

to begin)

Old Man

When the world was in the making,

Here within the mighty forest,

Came the Sun Man every morning.

White and shining was the Sun Man,

Blue his eyes were as the sky-blue,

Bright his hair was as dry grass is,

Warm his eyes were as the sun is,

Fruit and flower were in his glances;

All he looked on grew and sprouted,

As these trees we see about us,

Mightiest trees in all the forest,

For the Sun Man looked upon them.

Where his glance fell grasses seeded,

Where his feet fell sprang upstarting—

Buckeye woods and hazel thickets,

Berry bushes, manzanita,

Till his pathway was a garden,

Flowing after like a river,

Laughing into bud and blossom.

There was never frost nor famine

And the Nishinam were happy,

Singing, dancing through the seasons,

Never cold and never hungered,

When the Sun Man lived among us.

But the foxes mean and cunning,

Hating Nishinam and all men,

Laid their snares within this forest,

Caught the Sun Man in the morning,

With their ropes of sinew caught him,

Bound him down to steal his wisdom

And become themselves bright Sun Men,

Warm of glance and fruitful-footed,

Masters of the frost and famine.

Swiftly the Coyote running

Came to aid the fallen Sun Man,

Swiftly killed the cunning foxes,

Swiftly cut the ropes of sinew,

Swiftly the Coyote freed him.

But the Sun Man in his anger,

Lightning flashing, thunder-throwing,

Loosed the frost and fanged the famine,

Thorned the bushes, pinched the berries,

Put the bitter in the buckeye,

Rocked the mountains to their summits,

Flung the hills into the valleys,

Sank the lakes and shoaled the rivers,

Poured the fresh sea in the salt sea,

Stamped his foot here in the forest,

Where the water burst from under

Heel that raised him into heaven—

Angry with the world forever

Rose the Sun Man into heaven.

Shaman

(Solemnly.)

I am the Shaman. I know what has gone

before and what will come after. I have passed

down through the gateway of death and talked

with the dead. My eyes have looked upon the

unseen things. My ears have heard the

unspoken words. And now I shall tell you of

the Sun Man in the days to come.

(Shaman stiffens suddenly with hideous

facial distortions, with inturned eye-balls

and loosened jaw. He waves his arms

about, writhes and twists in torment, as

if in epilepsy.)

(The Women break into a wailing, inarticulate

chant, swaying their bodies to the

accent. The men join them somewhat

reluctantly, all save Red Cloud, who

betrays vexation, and War Chief, who

betrays truculence.)

(Shaman, leading the rising frenzy, with
convulsive shiverings and tremblings tears
of his skin garments so that he is quite
naked save for a girdle of eagle-claws
about his thighs. His long black hair
flies about his face. With an abruptness
that is startling, he ceases all movement
and stands erect, rigid. This is greeted
with a low moaning that slowly dies
away.)

CHANT OF PROPHECY

Shaman

The Sun never grows cold.

The Sun Man is like the Sun.

His anger never grows cold.

The Sun Man will return.

The Sun Man will come back from the Sun.

People

The Sun Man will return.

The Sun Man will come back from the Sun.

Shaman

There is a sign.

As the water burst forth when he rose into the sky,

So will the water cease to flow when he returns from the sky.

The Sun Man is mighty.

In his eyes is blue fire.

In his hands he bears the thunder.

The lightnings are in his hair.

People

In his hands he bears the thunder.

The lightnings are in his hair.

Shaman

There is a sign.

The Sun Man is white.

His skin is white like the sun.

His hair is bright like the sunlight.'

His eyes are blue like the sky.

People

There is a sign.

The Sun Man is white.

Shaman

The Sun Man is mighty.

He is the enemy of the Nishinam.

He will destroy the Nishinam.

People

He is the enemy of the Nishinam.

He will destroy the Nishinam.

Shaman

There is a sign.

The Sun Man will bear the thunder in his hand.

People

There is a sign.

The Sun Man will bear the thunder in his hand.

Shaman

In the day the Sun Man comes

The water from the spring will no longer flow.

And in that day he will destroy the Nishinam.

With the thunder will he destroy the Nishinam.

The Nishinam will be like last year's grasses.

The Nishinam will be like the smoke of last year's campfires.

The Nishinam will be less than the dreams that trouble the sleeper.

The Nishinam will be like the days no man remembers.

I am the Shaman.

I have spoken.

(The People set up a sad wailing.)

War Chief

(Striking his chest with his fist.)

Hoh! Hoh! Hoh!

(The People cease from their wailing and

look to the War Chief with hopeful

expectancy.)

War Chief

I am the War Chief. In war I command.

Nor the Shaman nor Red Cloud may say me nay

when in war I command. Let the Sun Man

come back. I am not afraid. If the foxes snared

him with ropes, then can I slay him with spear-

thrust and war-club. I am the War Chief. In

war I command.

(The People greet War Chief's pronouncement

with warlike cries of approval.)

Red Cloud

The foxes are cunning. If they snared the Sun Man

With ropes of sinew, then let us be cunning

And snare him with ropes of kindness.

In kindness, O War Chief, is strength, much strength.

Shaman

Red Cloud speaks true. In kindness is strength.

War Chief

I am the War Chief.

Shaman

You cannot slay the Sun Man.

War Chief

I am the War Chief.

Shaman

The Sun Man fights with the thunder in his hand.

War Chief

I am the War Chief.

Red Cloud

(As he speaks the People are visibly wan by

his argument.)

You speak true, O War Chief. In war you

command. You are strong, most strong. You

have slain the Modoc. You have slain the Napa.

You have slain the Clam-Eaters of the big water

till the last one is not. Yet you have not slain

all the foxes. The foxes cannot fight, yet are

they stronger than you because you cannot slay

them. The foxes are foxes, but we are men.

When the Sun Man comes we will not be cunning

like the foxes. We will be kind. Kindness and

love will we give to the Sun Man, so that he will

be our friend. Then will he melt the frost, pull

the teeth of famine, give us back our rivers of

deep water, our lakes of sweet water, take the

bitter from the buckeye, and in all ways make

the world the good world it was before he left us.

People

Hail, Red Cloud, the first man!

Hail, Red Cloud, the Acorn-Planter!

Who showed us the way of our feet in the world!

Who showed us the way of our food in the world!

Who showed us the way of our hearts in the world!

Who gave us the law of family,

The law of tribe,

The law of totem,

And made us strong in the world among men!

(While the People sing the hillside slowly

grows dark.)

ACT I

(Ten thousand years have passed, and it is

the time of the early voyaging from Europe

to the waters of the Pacific, when the

deserted hillside is again revealed as the

moon rises. The stream no longer flows

from the spring. Since the grove is used

only as a camp for the night when the

Nishinam are on their seasonal migration

there are no signs of previous camps.)

(Enter from right, at end of day's march,
women, old men, and Shaman, the
women bending under their burdens of
camp gear and dunnage)

(Enter from left youths carrying fish-spears
and large fish)

(Appear, coming down the hillside, Red
Cloud and the hunters, many carrying
meat.)

(The various repeated characters, despite
differences of skin garmenting and decoration,
resemble their prototypes of the prologue.)

Red Cloud

Good hunting! Good hunting!

Hunters

Good hunting! Good hunting!

Youths

Good fishing! Good fishing!

Women

Good berries! Good acorns!

(The women and youths and hunters, as they
reach the campsite, begin throwing down

their burdens)

Dew-Woman

(Discovering the dry spring.)

The water no longer flows!

Shaman

(Stilling the excitement that is immediate

on the discovery.)

The word of old time that has come down to

us from all the Shamans who have gone before!

The Sun Man has come back from the Sun.

Dew-Woman

(Looking to Red Cloud.)

Let Red Cloud speak. Since the morning of

the world has Red Cloud ever been reborn with

the ancient wisdom to guide us.

War Chief

Save in war. In war I command.

(He picks out hunters by name.)

Deer Foot... Elk Man... Antelope. Run

through the forest, climb the hill-tops, seek down

the valleys, for aught you may find of this Sun Man.

(At a wave of the War Chief's hand the

three hunters depart in different directions.)

Dew-Woman

Let Red Cloud speak his mind.

Red Cloud

(Quietly)

Last night the earth shook and there was a roaring in the air. Often have I seen, when the earth shakes and there is a roaring, that springs in some places dry up, and that in other places where were no springs, springs burst forth.

Shaman

There is a sign.

The Shamans told it of old.

The Sun Man will bear the thunder in his hand.

People

There is a sign.

The Sun Man will bear the thunder in his hand.

Shaman

The roaring in the air was the thunder of the Sun Man's return. Now will he destroy the Nishinam. Such is the word.

War Chief

Hoh! Hoh!

(From right Deer Foot runs in.)

Deer Foot

(Breathless.)

They come! He comes!

War Chief

Who comes?

Deer Foot

The Sun Men. The Sun Man. He is their

chief. He marches before them. And he is

white.

People

There is a sign.

The Sun Man is white.

Red Cloud

Carries he the thunder in his hand?

Deer Foot

(Puzzled)

He looks hungry.

War Chief

Hoh! Hoh! The Sun Man is hungry. It

will be easy to kill a hungry Sun Man.

Red Cloud

It would be easy to be kind to a hungry Sun

Man and give him food. We have much. The

hunting has been good.

War Chief

Better to kill the Sun Man.

(He turns upon People, indicating most
commands in gestures as he prepares the
ambush, making women and boys conceal
all the camp outfit and game, and
disposing the armed hunters among the
ferns and behind trees till all are hidden.)

Elk Man and Antelope

(Running down hillside)

The Sun Man comes.

(War Chief sends them to hiding places)

War Chief

(Preparing himself to hide)

You have not hidden, O Red Cloud.

Red Cloud

(Stepping into shadow of big tree where he
remains inconspicuous though dimly
visible)

I would see this Sun Man and talk with him.

(The sound of singing is heard, and War
Chief conceals himself)

(Sun Man, with handful of followers, singing

to ease the tedium of the march, enter

from right. They are patently survivors

of a wrecked exploring skip, making their

way inland)

Sun Men

We sailed three hundred strong

   For the far Barbaree;

Our voyage has been most long

   For the far Barbaree;

     So—it's a long pull,

     Give a strong pull,

For the far Barbaree.

We sailed the oceans wide

   For the coast of Barbaree;

And left our ship a sinking

   On the coast of Barbaree;

     So—it's a long pull,

     Give a strong pull,

   For the far Barbaree.

Our ship went fast a-lee

   On the rocks of Barbaree;

That's why we quit the sea

On the rocks of Barbaree.

So—it's a long pull,

Give a strong pull,

For the far Barbaree.

We quit the bitter seas

On the coast of Barbaree;

To seek the savag-ees

Of the far Barbaree.

So—it's a long pull,

Give a strong pull,

For the far Barbaree.

Our feet are lame and sore

In the far Barbaree;

From treading of the shore

Of the far Barbaree.

So—it's a long pull,

Give a strong pull,

For the far Barbaree.

A weary brood are we

In the far Barbaree;

Sea cunies of the sea

In the far Barbaree.

So—it's a long pull,

Give a strong pull,

For the far Barbaree.

Sun Man

(Who alone carries a musket, and who is

evidently captain of the wrecked company)

No farther can we go this night. Mayhap

to-morrow we may find the savages and food.

(He glances about.)

This far world grows noble trees. We shall sleep

as in a temple.

First Sea Cuny

(Espying Red Cloud, and pointing.)

Look, Captain!

Sun Man

(Making the universal peace-sign, arm

raised and out, palm-outward.)

Who are you? Speak. We come in peace.

We kindness seek.

Red Cloud

(Advancing out of the shadow.)

Whence do you come?

Sun Man

From the great sea.

Red Cloud

I do not understand. No one journeys

on the great sea.

Sun Man

We have journeyed many moons.

Red Cloud

Have you come from the sun?

Sun Man

God wot! We have journeyed across the

sun, high and low in the sky, and over the sun

and under the sun the round world 'round.

Red Cloud

(With conviction.)

You come from the Sun. Your hair is like

the summer sunburnt grasses. Your eyes are

blue. Your skin is white.

(With absolute conviction.)

You are the Sun Man.

Sun Man

(With a shrug of shoulders.)

Have it so. I come from the Sun. I am the

Sun Man.

Red Cloud

Do you carry the thunder in your hand?

Sun Man

(Nonplussed for the moment, glances at

his musket, then smiles.)

Yes, I carry the thunder in my hand.

(War Chief and the Hunters leap

suddenly from ambush. Sun Man

warns Sea Cunies not to resist. War

Chief captures and holds Sun Man,

and Sea Cunies are similarly captured

and held. Women and boys appear, and

examine prisoners curiously.)

War Chief

Hoh! Hoh! Hoh! I have captured the

Sun Man! Like the foxes, I have captured

the Sun Man!—Deer Foot! Elk Man! The

foxes held the Sun Man. I now hold the Sun

Man. Then can you hold the Sun Man.

(Deer Foot and Elk Man seize the Sun

Man.)

Red Cloud

(To Shaman.)

He said he came in kindness.

War Chief

(Sneering.)

In kindness, with the thunder in his hand.

Shaman

(Deflected to partisanship of War Chief

by War Chief's success.)

By his own lips has he said it, with the thunder

in his hand.

War Chief

You are the Sun Man.

Sun Man

(Shrugging shoulders.)

My names are many as the stars. Call me

White Man.

Red Cloud

I am Red Cloud, the first man.

Sun Man

Then am I Adam, the first man and your

brother.

(Glancing about.)

And this is Eden, to look upon it.

Red Cloud

My father was the Coyote.

Sun Man

My father was Jehovah.

Red Cloud

I am the Fire-Bringer. I stole the fire from

the ground squirrel and hid it in the heart of

the wood.

Sun Man

Then am I Prometheus, your brother. I

stole the fire from heaven and hid it in the heart

of the wood.

Red Cloud

I am the Acorn-Planter. I am the Food-

Bringer, the Life-Maker. I make food for

more life, ever more life.

Sun Man

Then am I truly your brother. Life-Maker

am I, tilling the soil in the sweat of my brow

from the beginning of time, planting all manner

of good seeds for the harvest.

(Looking sharply at Red Cloud's skin

garments.)

Also am I the Weaver and Cloth-Maker.

(Holding out arm so that Red Cloud may

examine the cloth of the coat)

From the hair of the goat and the wool of

the sheep, and from beaten and spun grasses,

do I make the cloth to keep man warm.

Shaman

(Breaking in boastfully.)

I am the Shaman. I know all secret things.

Sun Man

I know my pathway under the sun over all

the seas, and I know the secrets of the stars

that show me my path where no path is. I

know when the Wolf of Darkness shall eat the

moon.

(Pointing toward moon.)

On this night shall the Wolf of Darkness eat

the moon.

(He turns suddenly to Red Cloud,

drawing sheath-knife and passing it

to him.)

More, O First Man and Acorn-Planter. I am

the Iron-Maker. Behold!

(Red Cloud examines knife, understands
immediately its virtue, cuts easily a strip
of skin from his skin garment, and is
overcome with the wonder of the knife.)

War Chief

(Exhibiting a long bow.)

I am the War Chief. No man, save me, has
strength to bend this bow. I can slay farther
than any man.

(A huge bear has come out among the
bushes far up the hillside)

Sun Man

I, too, am War Chief over men, and I can
slay farther than you.

War Chief

Hoh! Hoh!

Sun Man

(Pointing to bear)

Can you slay that with your strong bow?

War Chief

(Dubiously)

It is a far shot. Too far. No man can slay
a great bear so far.

(Sun Man, shaking off from his arms the

hands of Deer Foot and Elk Man,

aims musket and fires. The bear falls,

and the Nishinam betray astonishment

and awe)

(At a quick signal from War Chief,

Sun Man is again seized. War Chief

takes away musket and examines it.)

Shaman

There is a sign.

People

There is a sign.

He carries the thunder in his hand.

He slays with the thunder in his hand.

He is the enemy of the Nishinam.

He will destroy the Nishinam.

Shaman

There is a sign.

People

There is a sign.

In the day the Sun Man comes,

The waters from the spring will no longer flow,

And in that day will he destroy the Nishinam.

War Chief

(Exhibiting musket.)

Hoh! Hoh! I have taken the Sun Man's

thunder.

Shaman

Now shall the Sun Man die that the Nishinam

may live.

Red Cloud

He is our brother. He, too, is an acorn-

planter. He has spoken.

Shaman

He is the Sun Man, and he is our eternal

enemy. He shall die.

War Chief

In war I command.

(To Hunters.)

Tie their feet with stout thongs that they

may not run. And then make ready with bow

and arrow to do the deed.

(Hunters obey, urging and thrusting the

Sea Cunies into a compact group behind

the Sun Man.)

Red Cloud

Shaman I am not.

I know not the secret things.

I say the things I know.

When you plant kindness you harvest kindness.

When you plant blood you harvest blood.

He who plants one acorn makes way for life.

He who slays one man slays the planter of a

thousand acorns.

Shaman

Shaman I am.

I see the dark future.

I see the Sun Man's death,

The journey he must take

Through thick and endless forest

Where lost souls wander howling

A thousand moons of moons.

People

Through thick and endless forest

Where lost souls wander howling

A thousand moons of moons.

(War Chief arranges Hunters with their

bows and arrows for the killing.)

Sun Man

(To Red Cloud.)

You will slay us?

Red Cloud

(Indicating War Chief.)

In war he commands.

Sun Man

(Addressing the Nishinam)

Nor am I a Shaman. But I will tell you true

things to be. Our brothers are acorn-planters,

cloth-weavers, iron-workers. Our brothers are

life-makers and masters of life. Many are our

brothers and strong. They will come after us.

Your First Man has spoken true words. When

you plant blood you harvest blood. Our brothers

will come to the harvest with the thunder

in their hands. There is a sign. This night,

and soon, will the Wolf of Darkness eat the

moon. And by that sign will our brothers come

on the trail we have broken.

(As final preparation for the killing is

completed, and as Hunters are arranged

with their bows and arrows,

Sun Man sings.)

Sun Man

Our brothers will come after,

　On our trail to farthest lands;

Our brothers will come after

　With the thunder in their hands.

Sun Men

　　Loud will be the weeping,

　　Red will be the reaping,

　　High will be the heaping

　Of the slain their law commands.

Sun Man

Givers of law, our brothers,

　This is the law they say:

Who takes the life of a brother

　Ten of the slayers shall pay.

Sun Men

Our brothers will come after,

　On our trail to farthest lands;

Our brothers will come after

　With the thunder in their hands.

　　Loud will be the weeping,

　　Red will be the reaping,

　　High will be the heaping

Of the slain their law commands.

Sun Man

Our brothers will come after

By the courses that we lay;

Many and strong our brothers,

Masters of life are they.

Sun Men

Our brothers will come after

On our trail to farthest lands;

Our brothers will come after

With the thunder in their hands.

Loud will be the weeping,

Red will be the reaping,

High will be the heaping

Of the slain their law commands.

Sun Man

Plowers of land, our brothers,

Of the hills and pleasant leas;

Under the sun our brothers

With their keels will plow the seas.

Sun Men

Our brothers will come after,

On our trail to farthest lands;

Our brothers will come after

With the thunder in their hands.

Loud will be the weeping,

Red will be the reaping,

High will be the heaping

Of the slain their law commands.

Sun Man

Mighty men are our brothers,

Quick to forgive and to wrath,

Sailing the seas, our brothers

Will follow us on our path.

Sun Men

Our brothers will come after,

On our trail to farthest lands;

Our brothers will come after

With the thunder in their hands.

Loud will be the weeping,

Red will be the reaping,

High will be the heaping

Of the slain their law commands.

(At signal from War Chief the arrows

are discharged, and repeatedly

discharged. The Sun Men fall. The War

Chief himself kills the Sun Man.)

(In what follows, Red Cloud and Dew-

Woman stand aside, taking no part.

Red Cloud is depressed, and at the

same time is overcome with the wonder

of the knife which he still holds.)

War Chief

(Brandishing musket and drifting stiff-

legged, as he sings, into the beginning

of a war dance of victory.)

Hoh! Hoh! Hoh!

I have slain the Sun Man!

Hoh! Hoh! Hoh!

I hold his thunder in my hand!

Hoh! Hoh! Hoh!

Greatest of War Chiefs am I!

Hoh! Hoh! Hoh!

I have slain the Sun Man!

(The dance grows wilder.)

(After a time the hillside begins to darken)

Dew-Woman

(Pointing to the moon entering eclipse)

Lo! The Wolf of Darkness eats the Moon!

(In consternation the dance is broken off

for the moment)

Shaman

(Reassuringly)

It is a sign.

The Sun Man is dead.

War Chief

(Recovering courage and resuming dance.)

Hoh! Hoh! Hoh!

The Sun Man is dead!

People

(Resuming dance.)

Hoh! Hoh! Hoh!

The Sun Man is dead!

(As darkness increases the dance grows

into a saturnalia, until complete darkness

settles down and hides the hillside.)

ACT II

(A hundred years have passed, when the
hillside and the Nishinam in their
temporary camp are revealed. The spring
is flowing, and Women are filling gourds
with water. Red Cloud and Dew-
Woman stand apart from their people.)

Shaman

(Pointing.)

There is a sign.

The spring lives.

The water flows from the spring

And all is well with the Nishinam.

People

There is a sign.

The spring lives.

The water flows from the spring.

War Chief

(Boastingly.)

Hoh! Hoh! Hoh!

All is well with the Nishinam.

Hoh! Hoh! Hoh!

It is I who have made all well with the Nishinam.

Hoh! Hoh! Hoh!

I led our young men against the Napa.

Hoh! Hoh! Hoh!

We left no man living of the camp.

Hoh! Hoh! Hoh!

Shaman

Great is our War Chief!

Good is war!

No more will the Napa hunt our meat.

No more will the Napa pick our berries.

No more will the Napa catch our fish.

People

No more will the Napa hunt our meat.

No more will the Napa pick our berries.

No more will the Napa catch our fish.

War Chief

Hoh! Hoh! Hoh!

The War Chiefs before me made all well with

the Nishinam.

Hoh! Hoh! Hoh!

The War Chief of long ago slew the Sun Man.

Hoh! Hoh! Hoh!

The Sun Man said his brothers would come after.

Hoh! Hoh! Hoh!

The Sun Man lied.

People

Hoh! Hoh! Hoh!

The Sun Man lied.

Hoh! Hoh! Hoh!

The Sun Man lied.

Shaman

(Derisively.)

Red Cloud is sick. He lives in dreams. Ever

he dreams of the wonders of the Sun Man.

Red Cloud

The Sun Man was strong. The Sun Man was

a life-maker. The Sun Man planted acorns,

and cut quickly with a knife not of bone nor

stone, and of grasses and hides made cunning

cloth that is better than all grasses and hides.

—Old Man, where is the cunning cloth that is

better than all grasses and hides?

Old Man

(Fumbling in his skin pouch for the doth.)

In the many moons aforetime,

Hundred moons and many hundred,

When the old man was the young man,

When the young man was the youngling,

Dragging branches for the campfire,

Stealing suet from the bear-meat,

Cause of trouble to his mother,

Came the Sun Man in the night-time.

I alone of all the Nishinam

Live to-day to tell the story;

I alone of all the Nishinam

Saw the Sun Man come among us,

Heard the Sun Man and his Sun Men

Sing their death-song here among us

Ere they died beneath our arrows,

War Chief's arrows sharp and feathered—

War Chief

(Interrupting braggartly.)

Hoh! Hoh! Hoh!

Old Man

(Producing cloth.)

And the Sun Man and his Sun Men

Wore nor hair nor hide nor birdskin.

Cloth they wore from beaten grasses

Woven like our willow baskets,

Willow-woven acorn baskets

Women make in acorn season.

(Old Man hands piece of cloth to Red

Cloud.)

Red Cloud

(Admiring cloth.)

The Sun Man was an acorn-planter, and we

killed the Sun Man. We were not kind. We

made a blood-debt. Blood-debts are not good.

Shaman

The Sun Man lied. His brothers did not come

after. There is no blood-debt when there is no

one to make us pay.

Red Cloud

He who plants acorns reaps food, and food is

life. He who sows war reaps war, and war is death.

People

(Encouraged by Shaman and War Chief

to drown out Red Cloud's voice.)

Hoh! Hoh! Hoh!

The Sun Man is dead!

Hoh! Hoh! Hoh!

The Sun Man and his Sun Men are dead!

Red Cloud

(Shaking his head.)

His brothers of the Sun are coming after.

I have reports.

(Red Cloud beckons one after another of

the young hunters to speak)

First Hunter

To the south, not far, I wandered and lived

with the Petaluma. With my eyes I did not

see, but it was told me by those whose eyes had

seen, that still to the south, not far, were many

Sun Men—war chiefs who carry the thunder in

their hands; cloth-makers and weavers of cloth

like to that in Red Cloud's hand; acorn-planters

who plant all manner of strange seeds that ripen

to rich harvests of food that is good. And there

had been trouble. The Petaluma had killed

Sun Men, and many Petaluma had the Sun Men

killed.

Second Hunter

To the east, not far, I wandered and lived with

the Solano. With my own eyes I did not see,

but it was told me by those whose eyes had seen,

that still to the east, not far, and just beyond the

lands of the Tule tribes, were many Sun Men—

war chiefs and cloth-makers and acorn-planters.

And there had been trouble. The Solano had

killed Sun Men, and many Solano had the Sun Men killed.

Third Hunter

To the north, and far, I wandered and lived

with the Klamath. With my own eyes I did

not see, but it was told me by those whose eyes

had seen, that still to the north, and far, were

many Sun Men—war chiefs and cloth-makers

and acorn-planters. And there had been trouble.

The Klamath had killed Sun Men, and many

Klamath had the Sun Men killed.

Fourth Hunter

To the west, not far, three days gone I

wandered, where, from the mountain, I looked

down upon the great sea. With my own eyes

I saw. It was like a great bird that swam upon

the water. It had great wings like to our great

trees here. And on its back I saw men, many

men, and they were Sun Men. With my own

eyes I saw.

Red Cloud

We shall be kind to the Sun Men when they

come among us.

War Chief

(Dancing stiff-legged.)

Hoh! Hoh! Hoh!

Let the Sun Men come!

Hoh! Hoh! Hoh!

We will kill the Sun Men when they come!

People

(As they join in the war dance.)

Hoh! Hoh! Hoh!

Let the Sun Men come!

Hoh! Hoh! Hoh!

We will kill the Sun Men when they come.

(The dance grows wilder, the Shaman and

War Chief encouraging it, while Red

Cloud and Dew-Woman stand sadly at

a distance.)

(Rifle shots ring out from every side. Up

the hillside appear Sun Men firing rifles.

The Nishinam reel to death from their

dancing.)

(Red Cloud shields Dew-Woman with

one arm about her, and with the other arm

makes the peace-sign)

(The massacre is complete, Dew-Woman

and Red Cloud being the last to fall.

Red Cloud, wounded, the sole survivor,

rests on his elbow and watches the Sun

Men assemble about their leader)

(The Sun Men are the type of pioneer

Americans who, even before the discovery

of gold, were already drifting across the

Sierras and down into Oregon and

California with their oxen and great wagons.

With here and there a Rocky Mountain

trapper or a buckskin-clad scout of the

Kit Carson type, in the main they are

backwoods farmers. All carry the long

rifle of the period.)

(The Sun Man is buckskin-clad, with long

blond hair sweeping his shoulders.)

Sun Men

(Led by Sun Man.)

We crossed the Western Ocean

Three hundred years ago,

We cleared New England's forests

Three hundred years ago.

Blow high, blow low,

Heigh hi, heigh ho,

We cleared New England's forests

Three hundred years ago.

We climbed the Alleghanies

Two hundred years ago,

We reached the Susquehanna

Two hundred years ago.

Blow high, blow low,

Heigh hi, heigh ho,

We reached the Susquehanna

Two hundred years ago.

We crossed the Mississippi

One hundred years ago,

And glimpsed the Rocky Mountains

One hundred years ago.

Blow high, blow low,

Heigh hi, heigh ho,

And glimpsed the Rocky Mountains

One hundred years ago.

We passed the Rocky Mountains

    A year or so ago,

And crossed the salty deserts

    A year or so ago.

    Blow high, blow low,

    Heigh hi, heigh ho,

And crossed the salty deserts

    A year or so ago.

We topped the high Sierras

    But a few days ago,

And saw great California

    But a few days ago.

    Blow high, blow low,

    Heigh hi, heigh ho,

And saw great California

    But a few days ago.

We crossed Sonoma's mountains

    An hour or so ago,

And found this mighty forest

    An hour or so ago.

    Blow high, blow low,

Heigh hi, heigh ho,

And found this mighty forest

An hour or so ago.

Sun Man

(Glancing about at the slain and at the giant

forest.)

Good the day, good the deed, and good this

California land.

Red Cloud

Not with these eyes, but with other eyes in my

lives before, have I beheld you. You are the

Sun Man.

(The attention of all is drawn to Red

Cloud, and they group about him and the

Sun Man.)

Sun Man

Call me White Man. Though in truth we

follow the sun. All our lives have we followed

the sunset sun, as our fathers followed it before

us.

Red Cloud

And you slay us with the thunder in your hand.

You slay us because we slew your brothers.

Sun Man

(Nodding to Red Cloud and addressing

his own followers)

You see, it was no mistake. He confesses it.

Other white men have they slain.

Red Cloud

There will come a day when men will not slay

men and when all men will be brothers. And in

that day all men will plant acorns.

Sun Man

You speak well, brother.

Red Cloud

Ever was I for peace, but in war I did not command.

Ever I sought the secrets of the growing

things, the times and seasons for planting. Ever

I planted acorns, making two black oak trees

grow where one grew before. And now all is

ended. Oh my black oak acorns! My black

oak acorns! Who will plant them now?

Sun Man

Be of good cheer. We, too, are planters.

Rich is your land here. Not from poor soil can

such trees sprout heavenward. We will plant

many seeds and grow mighty harvests.

Red Cloud

I planted the short acorns in the valley. I
planted the long acorns in the valley. I made
food for life.

Sun Man

You planted well, brother, but not well enough.
It is for that reason that you pass. Your fat
valley grows food but for a handful of men. We
shall plant your fat valley and grow food for ten
thousand men.

Red Cloud

Ever I counseled peace and planting.

Sun Man

Some day all men will counsel peace. No
man will slay his fellow. All men will plant.

Red Cloud

But before that day you will slay, as you have
this day slain us?

Sun Man

You killed our brothers first. Blood-debts must
be paid. It is man's way upon the earth. But
more, O brother! We follow the sunset sun, and
the way before us is red with war. The way

behind us is white with peace. Ever, before

us, we make room for life. Ever we slay the

squalling crawling things of the wild. Ever we

clear the land and destroy the weeds that block

the way of life for the seeds we plant. We are

many, and many are our brothers that come after

along the way of peace we blaze. Where you

make two black oaks grow in the place of one,

we make an hundred. And where we make one

grow, our brothers who come after make an

hundred hundred.

Red Cloud

Truly are you the Sun Man. We knew about

you of old time. Our old men knew and sang of

you:

White and shining was the Sun Man,

Blue his eyes were as the sky-blue,

Bright his hair was as dry grass is,

Warm his eyes were as the sun is,

Fruit and flower were in his glances,

All he looked on grew and sprouted,

Where his glance fell grasses seeded,

Where his feet fell sprang upstarting

Buckeye woods and hazel thickets,

Berry bushes, manzanita,

Till his pathway was a garden,

Flowing after like a river

Laughing into bud and blossom.

SONG OF THE PIONEERS

Sun Men

Our brothers follow on the trail we blaze.

  Where howled the wolf and ached the naked plain

    Spring bounteous harvests at our brothers' hands;

In place of war's alarums, peaceful days;

  Above the warrior's grave the golden grain

    Turns deserts grim and stark to laughing lands.

Sun Man

We cleared New England's flinty slopes and plowed

Her rocky fields to fairness in the sun,

But fared we westward always for we sought

A land of golden richness and we knew

The land was waiting on the sunset trail.

Where we found forest we left fertile fields,

We bridled rivers wild to grind our corn,

The deer-paths turned to roadways at our heels,

Our axes felled the trees that bridged the streams,

And fenced the meadow pastures for our kine.

Sun Men

Our brothers follow on the trail we blaze;

   Where howled the wolf and ached the naked plain

   Spring bounteous harvests at our brothers' hands;

In place of war's alarums, peaceful days;

   Above the warrior's grave the golden grain

     Turns deserts grim and stark to laughing lands.

Sun Man

Beyond the Mississippi still we fared,

And rested weary by the River Platte

Until the young grass velveted the Plains,

Then yoked again our oxen to the trail

That ever led us west to farthest west.

Our women toiled beside us, and our young,

And helped to break the soil and plant the corn,

And fought beside us in the battle front

To fight of arrow, whine of bullet, when

We chained our circled wagons wheel to wheel.

Sun Men

Our brothers follow on the trail we blaze;

   Where howled the wolf and ached the naked plain

     Spring bounteous harvests at our brothers hands;

In place of war's alarums, peaceful days;

Above the warrior's grave the golden grain

Turns deserts grim and stark to laughing lands.

Sun Man

The rivers sank beneath the desert sand,

The tall pines dwarfed to sage-brush, and the grass

Grew sparse and bitter in the alkali,

But fared we always toward the setting sun.

Our oxen famished till the last one died

And our great wagons rested in the snow.

We climbed the high Sierras and looked down

From winter bleak upon the land we sought,

A sunny land, a rich and fruitful land,

The warm and golden California land.

Sun Men

Our brothers follow on the trail we blaze;

Where howled the wolf and ached the naked plain

Spring bounteous harvests at our brothers' hands;

In place of war's alarums, peaceful days;

Above the warrior's grave the golden grain

Turns deserts grim and stark to laughing lands.

(The hillside begins to darken.)

Red Cloud

(Faintly.)

The darkness is upon me. You are acorn-

planters. You are my brothers. The darkness

is upon me and I pass.

Sun Men

(As total darkness descends.)

Our brothers follow on the trail we blaze;

   Where howled the wolf and ached the naked plain

     Spring bounteous harvests at our brothers' hands;

In place of war's alarums, peaceful days;

   Above the warrior's grave the golden grain

     Turns deserts grim and stark to laughing lands.

EPILOGUE

Red Cloud

Good tidings! Good tidings

To the sons of men!

Good tidings! Good tidings!

War is dead!

(Light begins to suffuse the hillside, revealing

Red Cloud far up the hillside in a

commanding position on an out-jut of

rock.)

Lo, the New Day dawns,

The day of brotherhood,

The day when all men

Shall be kind to all men,

And all men shall be sowers of life.

(From every side a burst of voices.)

Hail to Red Cloud!

The Acorn-Planter!

The Life-Maker!

Hail! All hail!

The New Day dawns,

The day of brotherhood,

The day of man.

(A band of Warriors appears on hillside.)

Warriors

Hail, Red Cloud!

Mightier than all fighting men!

The slayer of War!

We are not sad.

Our eyes were blinded.

We did not know one acorn planted

Was mightier than an hundred fighting men.

We are not sad.

Our red work was when

The world was young and wild.

The world has grown wise.

No man slays his brother.

Our work is done.

In the light of the new day are we glad.

(A band of Pioneers and Sea Explorers

appears.)

Pioneers and Explorers

Hail, Red Cloud!

The first planter!

The Acorn-Planter!

We sang that War would die,

The anarch of our wild and wayward past.

We sang our brothers would come after,

Turning desert into garden,

Sowing friendship, and not hatred,

Planting seeds instead of dead men,

Growing men to manhood in the sun.

(A band of Husbandmen appear, bearing

fruit and sheaves of grain and corn.)

Husbandmen

Hail, Red Cloud!

The first planter!

The Acorn-Planter!

The harvests no more are red, but golden,

We are thy children.

We plant for increase,

Increase of wheat and corn,

Of fruit and flower,

Of sheep and kine,

Of love and lovers;

Rich are our harvests

And many are our lovers.

Red Cloud

Death is a stench in the nostrils,

Life is beauty and joy.

The planters are ever brothers.

Never are the warriors brothers;

Their ways are set apart,

Their hands raised each against each.

The planters' ways are the one way.

Ever they plant for life,

For life more abundant,

For beauty of head and hand,

For the voices of children playing,

And the laughter of maids in the twilight

And the lover's song in the gloom.

All Voices

Hail, Red Cloud!

The first planter!

The Acorn-Planter!

The maker of life!

Hail! All hail!

The New Day dawns,

The day of brotherhood,

The day of man!

THE END

**STORIES OF SHIPS AND
THE SEA: LITTLE BLUE
BOOK #1169**

CHRIS FARRINGTON: ABLE SEAMAN

"If you vas in der old country ships, a liddle shaver like you vood pe only der boy, und you vood wait on der able seamen. Und ven der able seaman sing out, 'Boy, der water-jug!' you vood jump quick, like a shot, und bring der water-jug. Und ven der able seaman sing out, 'Boy, my boots!' you vood get der boots. Und you vood pe politeful, und say 'Yessir' und 'No sir.' But you pe in der American ship, and you t'ink you are so good as der able seamen. Chris, mine boy, I haf ben a sailorman for twenty-two years, und do you t'ink you are so good as me? I vas a sailorman pefore you vas borned, und I knot und reef und splice ven you play mit topstrings und fly kites."

"But you are unfair, Emil!" cried Chris Farrington, his sensitive face flushed and hurt. He was a slender though strongly built young fellow of seventeen, with Yankee ancestry writ large all over him.

"Dere you go vonce again!" the Swedish sailor exploded. "My name is Mister Johansen, und a kid of a boy like you call me 'Emil!' It vas insulting, und comes pecause of der American ship!"

"But you call me 'Chris'!" the boy expostulated, reproachfully.

"But you vas a boy."

"Who does a man's work," Chris retorted. "And because I do a man's work I have as much right to call you by your first name as you me. We are all equals in this fo'castle, and you know it. When we signed for the voyage in San Francisco, we signed as sailors on the *Sophie Sutherland* and there was no difference made with any of us. Haven't I always done my work? Did I ever shirk? Did you or any other man ever have to take a wheel for me? Or a lookout? Or go aloft?"

"Chris is right," interrupted a young English sailor. "No man has had to do a tap of his work yet. He signed as good as any of us and he's shown himself as good—"

"Better!" broke in a Novia Scotia man. "Better than some of us! When we struck the sealing-grounds he turned out to be next to the best boat-steerer aboard. Only French Louis, who'd been at it for years, could beat him. I'm only a boat-puller, and you're only a boat-puller, too, Emil Johansen, for all your twenty-two years at sea. Why don't you become a boat-steerer?"

"Too clumsy," laughed the Englishman, "and too slow."

"Little that counts, one way or the other," joined in Dane Jurgensen, coming to the aid of his Scandinavian brother. "Emil is a man grown and an able seaman; the boy is neither."

And so the argument raged back and forth, the Swedes, Norwegians and Danes, because of race kinship, taking the part of Johansen, and the English, Canadians and Americans taking the part of Chris. From an unprejudiced point of view, the right was on the side of Chris. As he had truly said, he did a man's work, and the same work that any of them did. But they were prejudiced, and badly so, and out of the words which passed rose a standing quarrel which divided the forecastle into two parties.

The *Sophie Sutherland* was a seal-hunter, registered out of San Francisco, and engaged in hunting the furry sea-animals along the Japanese coast north to Bering Sea. The other vessels were two-masted schooners, but she was a three-master and the largest in the fleet. In fact, she was a full-rigged, three-topmast schooner, newly built.

Although Chris Farrington knew that justice was with him, and that he performed all his work faithfully and well, many a time, in secret thought, he longed for some pressing emergency to arise whereby he could demonstrate to the Scandinavian seamen that he also was an able seaman.

But one stormy night, by an accident for which he was in nowise accountable, in overhauling a spare anchor-chain he had all the fingers of his left hand badly crushed. And his hopes were likewise crushed, for it was impossible for him to continue hunting with the boats, and he was forced to stay idly aboard until his fingers should heal. Yet, although he little dreamed it, this very accident was to give him the long-looked-for-opportunity.

One afternoon in the latter part of May the *Sophie Sutherland* rolled sluggishly in a breathless calm. The seals were abundant, the hunting good, and the boats were all away and out of sight. And with them was almost every man of the crew. Besides Chris, there remained only the captain, the sailing-master and the Chinese cook.

The captain was captain only by courtesy. He was an old man, past eighty, and blissfully ignorant of the sea and its ways; but he was the owner of the vessel, and hence the honorable title. Of course the sailing-master, who was really captain, was a thorough-going seaman. The mate, whose post was aboard, was out with the boats, having temporarily taken Chris's place as boat-steerer.

When good weather and good sport came together, the boats were accustomed to range far and wide, and often did not return to the schooner until long after dark. But for all that it was a perfect hunting day, Chris noted a growing anxiety on the part of the sailing-master. He paced the deck nervously, and was constantly sweeping the horizon with his marine glasses. Not a boat was in sight. As sunset arrived, he even sent Chris aloft to the mizzen-topmast-head, but with no better luck. The boats could not possibly be back before midnight.

Since noon the barometer had been falling with startling rapidity, and all the signs were ripe for a great storm—how great, not even the sailing-master anticipated. He and Chris set to work to prepare for it. They put storm gaskets on the furled topsails, lowered and stowed the foresail and spanker and took in the two inner jibs. In the one remaining jib they put a single reef, and a single reef in the mainsail.

Night had fallen before they finished, and with the darkness came the storm. A low moan swept over the sea, and the wind struck the *Sophie Sutherland* flat. But she righted quickly, and with the sailing-master at the wheel, sheered her bow into within five points of the wind. Working as well as he could with his bandaged hand, and with the feeble aid of the Chinese cook, Chris went forward and backed the jib over to the weather side. This with the flat mainsail, left the schooner hove to.

"God help the boats! It's no gale! It's a typhoon!" the sailing-master shouted to Chris at eleven o'clock. "Too much canvas! Got to get two more reefs into the mainsail, and got to do it right away!" He glanced at the old captain, shivering in oilskins at the binnacle and holding on for dear life. "There's only you and I, Chris—and the cook; but he's next to worthless!"

In order to make the reef, it was necessary to lower the mainsail, and the removal of this after pressure was bound to make the schooner fall off before the wind and sea because of the forward pressure of the jib.

"Take the wheel!" the sailing-master directed. "And when I give the word, hard up with it! And when she's square before it, steady her! And keep her there! We'll heave to again as soon as I get the reefs in!"

Gripping the kicking spokes, Chris watched him and the reluctant cook go forward into the howling darkness. The *Sophie Sutherland* was plunging into the huge head-seas and wallowing tremendously, the tense steel stays and taut rigging humming like harp-strings to the wind. A buffeted cry came to his ears, and he felt the schooner's bow paying off of its own accord. The mainsail was down!

He ran the wheel hard-over and kept anxious track of the changing direction of the wind on his face and of the heave of the vessel. This was the crucial moment. In performing the evolution she would have to pass broadside to the surge before she could get before it. The wind was blowing directly on his right cheek, when he felt the *Sophie Sutherland* lean over and begin to rise toward the sky—up—up—an infinite distance! Would she clear the crest of the gigantic wave?

Again by the feel of it, for he could see nothing, he knew that a wall of water was rearing and curving far above him along the whole weather side. There was an instant's calm as the liquid wall intervened and shut off the wind. The schooner righted, and for that instant seemed at perfect rest. Then she rolled to meet the descending rush.

Chris shouted to the captain to hold tight, and prepared himself for the shock. But the man did not live who could face it. An ocean of water smote

Chris's back and his clutch on the spokes was loosened as if it were a baby's. Stunned, powerless, like a straw on the face of a torrent, he was swept onward he knew not whither. Missing the corner of the cabin, he was dashed forward along the poop runway a hundred feet or more, striking violently against the foot of the foremast. A second wave, crushing inboard, hurled him back the way he had come, and left him half-drowned where the poop steps should have been.

Bruised and bleeding, dimly conscious, he felt for the rail and dragged himself to his feet. Unless something could be done, he knew the last moment had come. As he faced the poop, the wind drove into his mouth with suffocating force. This brought him back to his senses with a start. The wind was blowing from dead aft! The schooner was out of the trough and before it! But the send of the sea was bound to breach her to again. Crawling up the runway, he managed to get to the wheel just in time to prevent this. The binnacle light was still burning. They were safe!

That is, he and the schooner were safe. As to the welfare of his three companions he could not say. Nor did he dare leave the wheel in order to find out, for it took every second of his undivided attention to keep the vessel to her course. The least fraction of carelessness and the heave of the sea under the quarter was liable to thrust her into the trough. So, a boy of one hundred and forty pounds, he clung to his herculean task of guiding the two hundred straining tons of fabric amid the chaos of the great storm forces.

Half an hour later, groaning and sobbing, the captain crawled to Chris's feet. All was lost, he whimpered. He was smitten unto death. The galley had gone by the board, the mainsail and running-gear, the cook, every thing!

"Where's the sailing-master?" Chris demanded when he had caught his breath after steadying a wild lurch of the schooner. It was no child's play to steer a vessel under single reefed jib before a typhoon.

"Clean up for'ard," the old man replied "Jammed under the fo'c'sle-head, but still breathing. Both his arms are broken, he says and he doesn't know how many ribs. He's hurt bad."

"Well, he'll drown there the way she's shipping water through the hawse-pipes. Go for'ard!" Chris commanded, taking charge of things as a matter of course. "Tell him not to worry; that I'm at the wheel. Help him as much as you can, and make him help"—he stopped and ran the spokes to starboard as a tremendous billow rose under the stern and yawed the schooner to port—"and make him help himself for the rest. Unship the fo'castle hatch and get him down into a bunk. Then ship the hatch again."

The captain turned his aged face forward and wavered pitifully. The waist of the ship was full of water to the bulwarks. He had just come through it, and knew death lurked every inch of the way.

"Go!" Chris shouted, fiercely. And as the fear-stricken man started, "And take another look for the cook!"

Two hours later, almost dead from suffering, the captain returned. He had obeyed orders. The sailing-master was helpless, although safe in a bunk; the cook was gone. Chris sent the captain below to the cabin to change his clothes.

After interminable hours of toil day broke cold and gray. Chris looked about him. The *Sophie Sutherland* was racing before the typhoon like a thing possessed. There was no rain, but the wind whipped the spray of the sea mast-high, obscuring everything except in the immediate neighborhood.

Two waves only could Chris see at a time—the one before and the one behind. So small and insignificant the schooner seemed on the long Pacific roll! Rushing up a maddening mountain, she would poise like a cockle-shell on the giddy summit, breathless and rolling, leap outward and down into the yawning chasm beneath, and bury herself in the smother of foam at the bottom. Then the recovery, another mountain, another sickening upward rush, another poise, and the downward crash. Abreast of him, to starboard, like a ghost of the storm, Chris saw the cook dashing apace with the schooner. Evidently, when washed overboard, he had grasped and become entangled in a trailing halyard.

For three hours more, alone with this gruesome companion, Chris held the *Sophie Sutherland* before the wind and sea. He had long since forgotten his mangled fingers. The bandages had been torn away, and the cold, salt spray had eaten into the half-healed wounds until they were numb and no longer pained. But he was not cold. The terrific labor of steering forced the perspiration from every pore. Yet he was faint and weak with hunger and exhaustion, and hailed with delight the advent on deck of the captain, who fed him all of a pound of cake-chocolate. It strengthened him at once.

He ordered the captain to cut the halyard by which the cook's body was towing, and also to go forward and cut loose the jib-halyard and sheet. When he had done so, the jib fluttered a couple of moments like a handkerchief, then tore out of the bolt-ropes and vanished. The *Sophie Sutherland* was running under bare poles.

By noon the storm had spent itself, and by six in the evening the waves had died down sufficiently to let Chris leave the helm. It was almost hopeless to dream of the small boats weathering the typhoon, but there is always the chance in saving human life, and Chris at once applied himself to going back over the course along which he had fled. He managed to get a reef in one of the inner jibs and two reefs in the spanker, and then, with the aid of the watch-tackle, to hoist them to the stiff breeze that yet blew. And all through the night, tacking back and forth on the back track, he shook out canvas as fast as the wind would permit.

The injured sailing-master had turned delirious and between tending him and lending a hand with the ship, Chris kept the captain busy. "Taught me more seamanship," as he afterward said, "than I'd learned on the whole voyage." But by daybreak the old man's feeble frame succumbed, and he fell off into exhausted sleep on the weather poop.

Chris, who could now lash the wheel, covered the tired man with blankets from below, and went fishing in the lazaretto for something to eat. But by the day following he found himself forced to give in, drowsing fitfully by the wheel and waking ever and anon to take a look at things.

On the afternoon of the third day he picked up a schooner, dismasted and battered. As he approached, close-hauled on the wind, he saw her decks crowded by an unusually large crew, and on sailing in closer, made out among others the faces of his missing comrades. And he was just in the nick of time, for they were fighting a losing fight at the pumps. An hour later they, with the crew of the sinking craft were aboard the *Sophie Sutherland*.

Having wandered so far from their own vessel, they had taken refuge on the strange schooner just before the storm broke. She was a Canadian sealer on her first voyage, and as was now apparent, her last.

The captain of the *Sophie Sutherland* had a story to tell, also, and he told it well—so well, in fact, that when all hands were gathered together on deck during the dog-watch, Emil Johansen strode over to Chris and gripped him by the hand.

"Chris," he said, so loudly that all could hear, "Chris, I gif in. You vas yoost so good a sailorman as I. You vas a bully boy und able seaman, und I pe proud for you!

"Und Chris!" He turned as if he had forgotten something, and called back, "From dis time always you call me 'Emil' mitout der 'Mister'!"

TYPHOON OFF THE COAST OF JAPAN

Jack London's First Story, Published at the Age of Seventeen.

It was four bells in the morning watch. We had just finished breakfast when the order came forward for the watch on deck to stand by to heave her to and all hands stand by the boats.

"Port! hard a port!" cried our sailing-master. "Clew up the topsails! Let the flying jib run down! Back the jib over to windward and run down the foresail!" And so was our schooner *Sophie Sutherland* hove to off the Japan coast, near Cape Jerimo, on April 10, 1893.

Then came moments of bustle and confusion. There were eighteen men to man the six boats. Some were hooking on the falls, others casting off the lashings; boat-steerers appeared with boat-compasses and water-breakers, and boat-pullers with the lunch boxes. Hunters were staggering under two or three shotguns, a rifle and heavy ammunition box, all of which were soon stowed away with their oilskins and mittens in the boats.

The sailing-master gave his last orders, and away we went, pulling three pairs of oars to gain our positions. We were in the weather boat, and so had a longer pull than the others. The first, second and third lee boats soon had all sail set and were running off to the southward and westward with the wind beam, while the schooner was running off to leeward of them, so that in case of accident the boats would have fair wind home.

It was a glorious morning, but our boat steerer shook his head ominously as he glanced at the rising sun and prophetically muttered: "Red sun in the morning, sailor take warning." The sun had an angry look, and a few light, fleecy "nigger-heads" in that quarter seemed abashed and frightened and soon disappeared.

Away off to the northward Cape Jerimo reared its black, forbidding head like some huge monster rising from the deep. The winter's snow, not yet entirely dissipated by the sun, covered it in patches of glistening white, over which the light wind swept on its way out to sea. Huge gulls rose slowly, fluttering their wings in the light breeze and striking their webbed feet on the surface of the water for over half a mile before they could leave it. Hardly had the patter, patter died away when a flock of sea quail rose, and with whistling wings flew away to windward, where members of a large band of whales were disporting themselves, their blowings sounding like the exhaust of steam engines. The harsh, discordant cries of a sea-parrot grated unpleasantly on the ear, and set half a dozen alert in a small band of seals that were ahead of us. Away they went, breaching and jumping entirely out of water. A sea-gull with slow, deliberate flight and long, majestic curves circled round us, and as a reminder of home a little English sparrow perched impudently on the fo'castle head, and, cocking his head on one side, chirped merrily. The boats were soon among the seals, and the bang! bang! of the guns could be heard from down to leeward.

The wind was slowly rising, and by three o'clock as, with a dozen seals in our boat, we were deliberating whether to go on or turn back, the recall flag was run up at the schooner's mizzen—a sure sign that with the rising wind the barometer was falling and that our sailing-master was getting anxious for the welfare of the boats.

Away we went before the wind with a single reef in our sail. With clenched teeth sat the boat-steerer, grasping the steering oar firmly with both hands, his restless eyes on the alert—a glance at the schooner ahead, as we rose on a sea, another at the mainsheet, and then one astern where the dark ripple of the wind on the water told him of a coming puff or a large white-cap that threatened to overwhelm us. The waves were holding high carnival, performing the strangest antics, as with wild glee they danced along in fierce pursuit—now up, now down, here, there, and everywhere, until some great sea of liquid green with its milk-white crest of foam rose from the ocean's throbbing bosom and drove the others from view. But only for a moment, for again under new forms they reappeared. In the sun's path they wandered, where every ripple, great or small, every little spit or spray looked like molten silver, where the water lost its dark green color and became a dazzling, silvery flood, only to vanish and become a wild waste of sullen turbulence, each dark foreboding sea rising and breaking, then rolling on again. The dash, the sparkle, the silvery light soon vanished with the sun, which became obscured by black clouds that were rolling swiftly in from the west, northwest; apt heralds of the coming storm.

We soon reached the schooner and found ourselves the last aboard. In a few minutes the seals were skinned, boats and decks washed, and we were down below by the roaring fo'castle fire, with a wash, change of clothes, and a hot, substantial supper before us. Sail had been put on the schooner, as we had a run of seventy-five miles to make to the southward before morning, so as to get in the midst of the seals, out of which we had strayed during the last two days' hunting.

We had the first watch from eight to midnight. The wind was soon blowing half a gale, and our sailing-master expected little sleep that night as he paced up and down the poop. The topsails were soon clewed up and made fast, then the flying jib run down and furled. Quite a sea was rolling by this time, occasionally breaking over the decks, flooding them and threatening to smash the boats. At six bells we were ordered to turn them over and put on storm lashings. This occupied us till eight bells, when we were relieved by the mid-watch. I was the last to go below, doing so just as the watch on deck was furling the spanker. Below all were asleep except our green hand, the "bricklayer," who was dying of consumption. The wildly dancing movements of the sea lamp cast a pale, flickering light through the fo'castle and turned to golden honey the drops of water on the yellow oilskins. In all the corners dark shadows seemed to come and go, while up in the eyes of her, beyond the pall bits, descending from deck to deck, where they seemed to lurk like some dragon at the cavern's mouth, it was dark as Erebus. Now and again, the light seemed to penetrate for a moment as the schooner rolled heavier than usual, only to recede, leaving it darker and blacker than before. The roar of the wind through the rigging came to the ear muffled like the distant rumble of a train crossing a trestle or the surf on the beach, while the loud crash of the seas on her weather bow seemed almost to rend the beams and planking asunder as it resounded through the fo'castle. The creaking and groaning of the timbers, stanchions, and bulkheads, as the strain the vessel was undergoing was felt, served to drown the groans of the dying man as he tossed uneasily in his bunk. The working of the foremast against the deck beams caused a shower of flaky powder to fall, and sent another sound mingling with the tumultuous storm. Small cascades of water streamed from the pall bits from the fo'castle head above, and, joining issue with the streams from the wet oilskins, ran along the floor and disappeared aft into the main hold.

At two bells in the middle watch—that is, in land parlance one o'clock in the morning;—the order was roared out on the fo'castle: "All hands on deck and shorten sail!"

Then the sleepy sailors tumbled out of their bunk and into their clothes, oilskins and sea-boots and up on deck. 'Tis when that order comes on cold, blustering nights that "Jack" grimly mutters: "Who would not sell a farm and go to sea?"

It was on deck that the force of the wind could be fully appreciated, especially after leaving the stifling fo'castle. It seemed to stand up against you like a wall, making it almost impossible to move on the heaving decks or to breathe as the fierce gusts came dashing by. The schooner was hove to under jib, foresail and mainsail. We proceeded to lower the foresail and make it fast. The night was dark, greatly impeding our labor. Still, though not a star or the moon could pierce the black masses of storm clouds that obscured the sky as they swept along before the gale, nature aided us in a measure. A soft light emanated from the movement of the ocean. Each mighty sea, all phosphorescent and glowing with the tiny lights of myriads of animalculae, threatened to overwhelm us with a deluge of fire. Higher and higher, thinner and thinner, the crest grew as it began to curve and overtop preparatory to breaking, until with a roar it fell over the bulwarks, a mass of soft glowing light and tons of water which sent the sailors sprawling in all directions and left in each nook and cranny little specks of light that glowed and trembled till the next sea washed them away, depositing new ones in their places. Sometimes several seas following each other with great rapidity and thundering down on our decks filled them full to the bulwarks, but soon they were discharged through the lee scuppers.

To reef the mainsail we were forced to run off before the gale under the single reefed jib. By the time we had finished the wind had forced up such a tremendous sea that it was impossible to heave her to. Away we flew on the wings of the storm through the muck and flying spray. A wind sheer to starboard, then another to port as the enormous seas struck the schooner astern and nearly broached her to. As day broke we took in the jib, leaving not a sail unfurled. Since we had begun scudding she had ceased to take the seas over her bow, but amidships they broke fast and furious. It was a dry storm in the matter of rain, but the force of the wind filled the air with fine spray, which flew as high as the crosstrees and cut the face like a knife, making it impossible to see over a hundred yards ahead. The sea was a dark lead color as with long, slow, majestic roll it was heaped up by the wind into liquid mountains of foam. The wild antics of the schooner were sickening as she forged along. She would almost stop, as though climbing a mountain, then rapidly rolling to right and left as she gained the summit of a huge sea, she steadied herself and paused for a moment as though affrighted at the yawning precipice before her. Like an avalanche, she shot forward and down as the sea astern struck her with the force of a thousand battering rams, burying her bow to the cat-heads in the milky foam at the bottom that came on deck in all directions—forward, astern, to right and left, through the hawse-pipes and over the rail.

The wind began to drop, and by ten o'clock we were talking of heaving her to. We passed a ship, two schooners and a four-masted barkentine under the smallest canvas, and at eleven o'clock, running up the spanker and jib, we hove her to, and in another hour we were beating back again against the aftersea under full sail to regain the sealing ground away to the westward.

Below, a couple of men were sewing the "bricklayer's" body in canvas preparatory to the sea burial. And so with the storm passed away the "bricklayer's" soul.

THE LOST POACHER

"But they won't take excuses. You're across the line, and that's enough. They'll take you. In you go, Siberia and the salt mines. And as for Uncle Sam, why, what's he to know about it? Never a word will get back to the States. 'The *Mary Thomas*,' the papers will say, 'the *Mary Thomas* lost with all hands. Probably in a typhoon in the Japanese seas.' That's what the papers will say, and people, too. In you go, Siberia and the salt mines. Dead to the world and kith and kin, though you live fifty years."

In such manner John Lewis, commonly known as the "sea-lawyer," settled the matter out of hand.

It was a serious moment in the forecastle of the *Mary Thomas*. No sooner had the watch below begun to talk the trouble over, than the watch on deck came down and joined them. As there was no wind, every hand could be spared with the exception of the man at the wheel, and he remained only for the sake of discipline. Even "Bub" Russell, the cabin-boy, had crept forward to hear what was going on.

However, it was a serious moment, as the grave faces of the sailors bore witness. For the three preceding months the *Mary Thomas* sealing schooner, had hunted the seal pack along the coast of Japan and north to Bering Sea. Here, on the Asiatic side of the sea, they were forced to give over the chase, or rather, to go no farther; for beyond, the Russian cruisers patrolled forbidden ground, where the seals might breed in peace.

A week before she had fallen into a heavy fog accompanied by calm. Since then the fog-bank had not lifted, and the only wind had been light airs and catspaws. This in itself was not so bad, for the sealing schooners are never in a hurry so long as they are in the midst of the seals; but the trouble lay in the fact that the current at this point bore heavily to the north. Thus the *Mary Thomas* had unwittingly drifted across the line, and every hour she was penetrating, unwillingly, farther and farther into the dangerous waters where the Russian bear kept guard.

How far she had drifted no man knew. The sun had not been visible for a week, nor the stars, and the captain had been unable to take observations in order to determine his position. At any moment a cruiser might swoop down and hale the crew away to Siberia. The fate of other poaching seal-hunters was too well known to the men of the *Mary Thomas*, and there was cause for grave faces.

"Mine friends," spoke up a German boat-steerer, "it vas a pad piziness. Shust as ve make a big catch, und all honest, somedings go wrong, und der Russians nab us, dake our skins and our schooner, und send us mit der anarchists to Siberia. Ach! a pretty pad piziness!"

"Yes, that's where it hurts," the sea lawyer went on. "Fifteen hundred skins in the salt piles, and all honest, a big pay-day coming to every man Jack of us, and then to be captured and lose it all! It'd be different if we'd been poaching, but it's all honest work in open water."

"But if we haven't done anything wrong, they can't do anything to us, can they?" Bub queried.

"It strikes me as 'ow it ain't the proper thing for a boy o' your age shovin' in when 'is elders is talkin'," protested an English sailor, from over the edge of his bunk.

"Oh, that's all right, Jack," answered the sea-lawyer. "He's a perfect right to. Ain't he just as liable to lose his wages as the rest of us?"

"Wouldn't give thruppence for them!" Jack sniffed back. He had been planning to go home and see his family in Chelsea when he was paid off, and he was now feeling rather blue over the highly possible loss, not only of his pay, but of his liberty.

"How are they to know?" the sea-lawyer asked in answer to Bub's previous question. "Here we are in forbidden water. How do they know but what we came here of our own accord? Here we are, fifteen hundred skins in the hold. How do they know whether we got them in open water or in the closed sea? Don't you see, Bub, the evidence is all against us. If you caught a man with his pockets full of apples like those which grow on your tree, and if you caught him in your tree besides, what'd you think if he told you he couldn't help it, and had just been sort of blown there, and that anyway those apples came from some other tree—what'd you think, eh?"

Bub saw it clearly when put in that light, and shook his head despondently.

"You'd rather be dead than go to Siberia," one of the boat-pullers said. "They put you into the salt-mines and work you till you die. Never see daylight again. Why, I've heard tell of one fellow that was chained to his mate, and that mate died. And they were both chained together! And if they send you to the quicksilver mines you get salivated. I'd rather be hung than salivated."

"Wot's salivated?" Jack asked, suddenly sitting up in his bunk at the hint of fresh misfortunes.

"Why, the quicksilver gets into your blood; I think that's the way. And your gums all swell like you had the scurvy, only worse, and your teeth get loose in your jaws. And big ulcers forms, and then you die horrible. The strongest man can't last long a-mining quicksilver."

"A pad piziness," the boat-steerer reiterated, dolorously, in the silence which followed. "A pad piziness. I vish I vas in Yokohama. Eh? Vot vas dot?"

The vessel had suddenly heeled over. The decks were aslant. A tin pannikin rolled down the inclined plane, rattling and banging. From above came the slapping of canvas and the quivering rat-tat-tat of the after leech of the loosely stretched foresail. Then the mate's voice sang down the hatch, "All hands on deck and make sail!"

Never had such summons been answered with more enthusiasm. The calm had broken. The wind had come which was to carry them south into safety. With a wild cheer all sprang on deck. Working with mad haste, they flung out topsails, flying jibs and staysails. As they worked, the fog-bank lifted and the black vault of heaven, bespangled with the old familiar stars, rushed into view. When all was shipshape, the *Mary Thomas* was lying gallantly over on her side to a beam wind and plunging ahead due south.

"Steamer's lights ahead on the port bow, sir!" cried the lookout from his station on the forecastle-head. There was excitement in the man's voice.

The captain sent Bub below for his night-glasses. Everybody crowded to the lee-rail to gaze at the suspicious stranger, which already began to loom up vague and indistinct. In those unfrequented waters the chance was one in a thousand that it could be anything else than a Russian patrol. The captain was still anxiously gazing through the glasses, when a flash of flame left the stranger's side, followed by the loud report of a cannon. The worst fears were confirmed. It was a patrol, evidently firing across the bows of the *Mary Thomas* in order to make her heave to.

"Hard down with your helm!" the captain commanded the steersman, all the life gone out of his voice. Then to the crew, "Back over the jib and foresail! Run down the flying jib! Clew up the foretopsail! And aft here and swing on to the main-sheet!"

The *Mary Thomas* ran into the eye of the wind, lost headway, and fell to courtesying gravely to the long seas rolling up from the west.

The cruiser steamed a little nearer and lowered a boat. The sealers watched in heartbroken silence. They could see the white bulk of the boat as it was slacked away to the water, and its crew sliding aboard. They could hear the creaking of the davits and the commands of the officers. Then the boat sprang away under the impulse of the oars, and came toward them. The wind had been rising, and already the sea was too rough to permit the frail craft to lie alongside the tossing schooner; but watching their chance, and taking advantage of the boarding ropes thrown to them, an officer and a couple of men clambered aboard. The boat then sheered off into safety and lay to its oars, a young midshipman, sitting in the stern and holding the yoke-lines, in charge.

The officer, whose uniform disclosed his rank as that of second lieutenant in the Russian navy went below with the captain of the *Mary Thomas* to look at the ship's papers. A few minutes later he emerged, and upon his sailors removing the hatch-covers, passed down into the hold with a lantern to inspect the salt piles. It was a goodly heap which confronted him—fifteen hundred fresh skins, the season's catch; and under the circumstances he could have had but one conclusion.

"I am very sorry," he said, in broken English to the sealing captain, when he again came on deck, "but it is my duty, in the name of the tsar, to seize your vessel as a poacher caught with fresh skins in the closed sea. The penalty, as you may know, is confiscation and imprisonment."

The captain of the *Mary Thomas* shrugged his shoulders in seeming indifference, and turned away. Although they may restrain all outward show, strong men, under unmerited misfortune, are sometimes very close to tears. Just then the vision of his little California home, and of the wife and two yellow-haired boys, was strong upon him, and there was a strange, choking sensation in his throat, which made him afraid that if he attempted to speak he would sob instead.

And also there was upon him the duty he owed his men. No weakness before them, for he must be a tower of strength to sustain them in misfortune. He had already explained to the second lieutenant, and knew the hopelessness of the situation. As the sea-lawyer had said, the evidence was all against him. So he turned aft, and fell to pacing up and down the poop of the vessel over which he was no longer commander.

The Russian officer now took temporary charge. He ordered more of his men aboard, and had all the canvas clewed up and furled snugly away. While this was being done, the boat plied back and forth between the two vessels, passing a heavy hawser, which was made fast to the great towing-bitts on the schooner's forecastle-head. During all this work the sealers stood about in sullen groups. It was madness to think of resisting, with the guns of a man-of-war not a biscuit-toss away; but they refused to lend a hand, preferring instead to maintain a gloomy silence.

Having accomplished his task, the lieutenant ordered all but four of his men back into the boat. Then the midshipman, a lad of sixteen, looking strangely mature and dignified in his uniform and sword, came aboard to take command of the captured sealer. Just as the lieutenant prepared to depart his eye chanced to alight upon Bub. Without a word of warning, he seized him by the arm and dropped him over the rail into the waiting boat; and then, with a parting wave of his hand, he followed him.

It was only natural that Bub should be frightened at this unexpected happening. All the terrible stories he had heard of the Russians served to make him fear them, and now returned to his mind with double force. To be captured by them was bad enough, but to be carried off by them, away from his comrades, was a fate of which he had not dreamed.

"Be a good boy, Bub," the captain called to him, as the boat drew away from the *Mary Thomas*'s side, "and tell the truth!"

"Aye, aye, sir!" he answered, bravely enough by all outward appearance. He felt a certain pride of race, and was ashamed to be a coward before these strange enemies, these wild Russian bears.

"Und be politeful!" the German boat-steerer added, his rough voice lifting across the water like a fog-horn.

Bub waved his hand in farewell, and his mates clustered along the rail as they answered with a cheering shout. He found room in the stern-sheets, where he fell to regarding the lieutenant. He didn't look so wild or bearish after all—very much like other men, Bub concluded, and the sailors were much the same as all other man-of-war's men he had ever known. Nevertheless, as his feet struck the steel deck of the cruiser, he felt as if he had entered the portals of a prison.

For a few minutes he was left unheeded. The sailors hoisted the boat up, and swung it in on the davits. Then great clouds of black smoke poured out of the funnels, and they were under way—to Siberia, Bub could not help but think. He saw the *Mary Thomas* swing abruptly into line as she took the pressure from the hawser, and her side-lights, red and green, rose and fell as she was towed through the sea.

Bub's eyes dimmed at the melancholy sight, but—but just then the lieutenant came to take him down to the commander, and he straightened up and set his lips firmly, as if this were a very commonplace affair and he were used to being sent to Siberia every day in the week. The cabin in which the commander sat was like a palace compared to the humble fittings of the *Mary Thomas*, and the commander himself, in gold lace and dignity, was a most august personage, quite unlike the simple man who navigated his schooner on the trail of the seal pack.

Bub now quickly learned why he had been brought aboard, and in the prolonged questioning which followed, told nothing but the plain truth. The truth was harmless; only a lie could have injured his cause. He did not know much, except that they had been sealing far to the south in open water, and that when the calm and fog came down upon them, being close to the line, they had drifted across. Again and again he insisted that they had not lowered a boat or shot a seal in the week they had been drifting about in the forbidden sea; but the commander chose to consider all that he said to be a tissue of falsehoods, and adopted a bullying tone in an effort to frighten the boy. He threatened and cajoled by turns, but failed in the slightest to shake Bub's statements, and at last ordered him out of his presence.

By some oversight, Bub was not put in anybody's charge, and wandered up on deck unobserved. Sometimes the sailors, in passing, bent curious glances upon him, but otherwise he was left strictly alone. Nor could he have attracted much attention, for he was small, the night dark, and the watch on deck intent on its own business. Stumbling over the strange decks, he made his way aft where he could look upon the side-lights of the *Mary Thomas*, following steadily in the rear.

For a long while he watched, and then lay down in the darkness close to where the hawser passed over the stern to the captured schooner. Once an officer came up and examined the straining rope to see if it were chafing, but Bub cowered away in the shadow undiscovered. This, however, gave him an idea which concerned the lives and liberties of twenty-two men, and which was to avert crushing sorrow from more than one happy home many thousand miles away.

In the first place, he reasoned, the crew were all guiltless of any crime, and yet were being carried relentlessly away to imprisonment in Siberia—a living death, he had heard, and he believed it implicitly. In the second place, he was a prisoner, hard and fast, with no chance to escape. In the third, it was possible for the twenty-two men on the *Mary Thomas* to escape. The only thing which bound them was a four-inch hawser. They dared not cut it at their end, for a watch was sure to be maintained upon it by their Russian captors; but at this end, ah! at his end—

Bub did not stop to reason further. Wriggling close to the hawser, he opened his jack-knife and went to work. The blade was not very sharp, and he sawed away, rope-yarn by rope-yarn, the awful picture of the solitary Siberian exile he must endure growing clearer and more terrible at every stroke. Such a fate was bad enough to undergo with one's comrades, but to face it alone seemed frightful. And besides, the very act he was performing was sure to bring greater punishment upon him.

In the midst of such somber thoughts, he heard footsteps approaching. He wriggled away into the shadow. An officer stopped where he had been working, half-stooped to examine the hawser, then changed his mind and straightened up. For a few minutes he stood there, gazing at the lights of the captured schooner, and then went forward again.

Now was the time! Bub crept back and went on sawing. Now two parts were severed. Now three. But one remained. The tension upon this was so great that it readily yielded. Splash the freed end went overboard. He lay quietly, his heart in his mouth, listening. No one on the cruiser but himself had heard.

He saw the red and green lights of the *Mary Thomas* grow dimmer and dimmer. Then a faint hallo came over the water from the Russian prize crew. Still nobody heard. The smoke continued to pour out of the cruiser's funnels, and her propellers throbbed as mightily as ever.

What was happening on the *Mary Thomas*? Bub could only surmise; but of one thing he was certain: his comrades would assert themselves and overpower the four sailors and the midshipman. A few minutes later he saw a small flash, and straining his ears heard the very faint report of a pistol. Then, oh joy! both the red and green lights suddenly disappeared. The *Mary Thomas* was retaken!

Just as an officer came aft, Bub crept forward, and hid away in one of the boats. Not an instant too soon. The alarm was given. Loud voices rose in command. The cruiser altered her course. An electric search-light began to throw its white rays across the sea, here, there, everywhere; but in its flashing path no tossing schooner was revealed.

111

Bub went to sleep soon after that, nor did he wake till the gray of dawn. The engines were pulsing monotonously, and the water, splashing noisily, told him the decks were being washed down. One sweeping glance, and he saw that they were alone on the expanse of ocean. The *Mary Thomas* had escaped. As he lifted his head, a roar of laughter went up from the sailors. Even the officer, who ordered him taken below and locked up, could not quite conceal the laughter in his eyes. Bub thought often in the days of confinement which followed that they were not very angry with him for what he had done.

He was not far from right. There is a certain innate nobility deep down in the hearts of all men, which forces them to admire a brave act, even if it is performed by an enemy. The Russians were in nowise different from other men. True, a boy had outwitted them; but they could not blame him, and they were sore puzzled as to what to do with him. It would never do to take a little mite like him in to represent all that remained of the lost poacher.

So, two weeks later, a United States man-of-war, steaming out of the Russian port of Vladivostok, was signaled by a Russian cruiser. A boat passed between the two ships, and a small boy dropped over the rail upon the deck of the American vessel. A week later he was put ashore at Hakodate, and after some telegraphing, his fare was paid on the railroad to Yokohama.

From the depot he hurried through the quaint Japanese streets to the harbor, and hired a sampan boatman to put him aboard a certain vessel whose familiar rigging had quickly caught his eye. Her gaskets were off, her sails unfurled; she was just starting back to the United States. As he came closer, a crowd of sailors sprang upon the forecastle head, and the windlass-bars rose and fell as the anchor was torn from its muddy bottom.

"'Yankee ship come down the ribber!'" the sea-lawyer's voice rolled out as he led the anchor song.

"'Pull, my bully boys, pull!'" roared back the old familiar chorus, the men's bodies lifting and bending to the rhythm.

Bub Russell paid the boatman and stepped on deck. The anchor was forgotten. A mighty cheer went up from the men, and almost before he could catch his breath he was on the shoulders of the captain, surrounded by his mates, and endeavoring to answer twenty questions to the second.

The next day a schooner hove to off a Japanese fishing village, sent ashore four sailors and a little midshipman, and sailed away. These men did not talk English, but they had money and quickly made their way to Yokohama. From that day the Japanese village folk never heard anything more about them, and they are still a much-talked-of mystery. As the Russian government never said anything about the incident, the United States is still ignorant of the whereabouts of the lost poacher, nor has she ever heard, officially, of the way in which some of her citizens "shanghaied" five subjects of the tsar. Even nations have secrets sometimes.

THE BANKS OF THE SACRAMENTO

"And it's blow, ye winds, heigh-ho,

For Cal-i-for-ni-o;

For there's plenty of gold so I've been told,

On the banks of the Sacramento!"

It was only a little boy, singing in a shrill treble the sea chantey which seamen sing the wide world over when they man the capstan bars and break the anchors out for "Frisco" port. It was only a little boy who had never seen the sea, but two hundred feet beneath him rolled the Sacramento. "Young" Jerry he was called, after "Old" Jerry, his father, from whom he had learned the song, as well as received his shock of bright-red hair, his blue, dancing eyes, and his fair and inevitably freckled skin.

For Old Jerry had been a sailor, and had followed the sea till middle life, haunted always by the words of the ringing chantey. Then one day he had sung the song in earnest, in an Asiatic port, swinging and thrilling round the capstan-circle with twenty others. And at San Francisco he turned his back upon his ship and upon the sea, and went to behold with his own eyes the banks of the Sacramento.

He beheld the gold, too, for he found employment at the Yellow Dream mine, and proved of utmost usefulness in rigging the great ore-cables across the river and two hundred feet above its surface.

After that he took charge of the cables and kept them in repair, and ran them and loved them, and became himself an indispensable fixture of the Yellow Dream mine. Then he loved pretty Margaret Kelly; but she had left him and Young Jerry, the latter barely toddling, to take up her last long sleep in the little graveyard among the great sober pines.

Old Jerry never went back to the sea. He remained by his cables, and lavished upon them and Young Jerry all the love of his nature. When evil days came to the Yellow Dream, he still remained in the employ of the company as watchman over the all but abandoned property.

But this morning he was not visible. Young Jerry only was to be seen, sitting on the cabin step and singing the ancient chantey. He had cooked and eaten his breakfast all by himself, and had just come out to take a look at the world. Twenty feet before him stood the steel drum round which the endless cable worked. By the drum, snug and fast, was the ore-car. Following with his eyes the dizzy flight of the cables to the farther bank, he could see the other drum and the other car.

The contrivance was worked by gravity, the loaded car crossing the river by virtue of its own weight, and at the same time dragging the empty car back. The loaded car being emptied, and the empty car being loaded with more ore, the performance could be repeated—a performance which had been repeated tens of thousands of times since the day Old Jerry became the keeper of the cables.

Young Jerry broke off his song at the sound of approaching footsteps. A tall, blue-shirted man, a rifle across the hollow of his arm, came out from the gloom of the pine-trees. It was Hall, watchman of the Yellow Dragon mine, the cables of which spanned the Sacramento a mile farther up.

"Yello, younker!" was his greeting. "What you doin' here by your lonesome?"

"Oh, bachin'," Jerry tried to answer unconcernedly, as if it were a very ordinary sort of thing. "Dad's away, you see."

"Where's he gone?" the man asked.

"San Francisco. Went last night. His brother's dead in the old country, and he's gone down to see the lawyers. Won't be back till tomorrow night."

So spoke Jerry, and with pride, because of the responsibility which had fallen to him of keeping an eye on the property of the Yellow Dream, and the glorious adventure of living alone on the cliff above the river and of cooking his own meals.

"Well, take care of yourself," Hall said, "and don't monkey with the cables. I'm goin' to see if I can pick up a deer in the Cripple Cow Cañon."

"It's goin' to rain, I think," Jerry said, with mature deliberation.

"And it's little I mind a wettin'," Hall laughed, as he strode away among the trees.

Jerry's prediction concerning rain was more than fulfilled. By ten o'clock the pines were swaying and moaning, the cabin windows rattling, and the rain driving by in fierce squalls. At half past eleven he kindled a fire, and promptly at the stroke of twelve sat down to his dinner.

No out-of-doors for him that day, he decided, when he had washed the few dishes and put them neatly away; and he wondered how wet Hall was and whether he had succeeded in picking up a deer.

At one o'clock there came a knock at the door, and when he opened it a man and a woman staggered in on the breast of a great gust of wind. They were Mr. and Mrs. Spillane, ranchers, who lived in a lonely valley a dozen miles back from the river.

"Where's Hall?" was Spillane's opening speech, and he spoke sharply and quickly.

Jerry noted that he was nervous and abrupt in his movements, and that Mrs. Spillane seemed laboring under some strong anxiety. She was a thin, washed-out, worked-out woman, whose life of dreary and unending toil had stamped itself harshly upon her face. It was the same life that had bowed her husband's shoulders and gnarled his hands and turned his hair to a dry and dusty gray.

"He's gone hunting up Cripple Cow," Jerry answered. "Did you want to cross?"

The woman began to weep quietly, while Spillane dropped a troubled exclamation and strode to the window. Jerry joined him in gazing out to where the cables lost themselves in the thick downpour.

It was the custom of the backwoods people in that section of country to cross the Sacramento on the Yellow Dragon cable. For this service a small toll was charged, which tolls the Yellow Dragon Company applied to the payment of Hall's wages.

"We've got to get across, Jerry," Spillane said, at the same time jerking his thumb over his shoulder in the direction of his wife. "Her father's hurt at the Clover Leaf. Powder explosion. Not expected to live. We just got word."

Jerry felt himself fluttering inwardly. He knew that Spillane wanted to cross on the Yellow Dream cable, and in the absence of his father he felt that he dared not assume such a responsibility, for the cable had never been used for passengers; in fact, had not been used at all for a long time.

"Maybe Hall will be back soon," he said.

Spillane shook his head, and demanded, "Where's your father?"

"San Francisco," Jerry answered, briefly.

Spillane groaned, and fiercely drove his clenched fist into the palm of the other hand. His wife was crying more audibly, and Jerry could hear her murmuring, "And daddy's dyin', dyin'!"

The tears welled up in his own eyes, and he stood irresolute, not knowing what he should do. But the man decided for him.

"Look here, kid," he said, with determination, "the wife and me are goin' over on this here cable of yours! Will you run it for us?"

Jerry backed slightly away. He did it unconsciously, as if recoiling instinctively from something unwelcome.

"Better see if Hall's back," he suggested.

"And if he ain't?"

Again Jerry hesitated.

"I'll stand for the risk," Spillane added. "Don't you see, kid, we've simply got to cross!"

Jerry nodded his head reluctantly.

"And there ain't no use waitin' for Hall," Spillane went on. "You know as well as me he ain't back from Cripple Cow this time of day! So come along and let's get started."

No wonder that Mrs. Spillane seemed terrified as they helped her into the ore-car—so Jerry thought, as he gazed into the apparently fathomless gulf beneath her. For it was so filled with rain and cloud, hurtling and curling in the fierce blast, that the other shore, seven hundred feet away, was invisible, while the cliff at their feet dropped sheer down and lost itself in the swirling vapor. By all appearances it might be a mile to bottom instead of two hundred feet.

"All ready?" he asked.

"Let her go!" Spillane shouted, to make himself heard above the roar of the wind.

He had clambered in beside his wife, and was holding one of her hands in his.

Jerry looked upon this with disapproval. "You'll need all your hands for holdin' on, the way the wind's yowlin'."

The man and the woman shifted their hands accordingly, tightly gripping the sides of the car, and Jerry slowly and carefully released the brake. The drum began to revolve as the endless cable passed round it, and the car slid slowly out into the chasm, its trolley wheels rolling on the stationary cable overhead, to which it was suspended.

It was not the first time Jerry had worked the cable, but it was the first time he had done so away from the supervising eye of his father. By means of the brake he regulated the speed of the car. It needed regulating, for at times, caught by the stronger gusts of wind, it swayed violently back and forth; and once, just before it was swallowed up in a rain squall, it seemed about to spill out its human contents.

After that Jerry had no way of knowing where the car was except by means of the cable. This he watched keenly as it glided around the drum. "Three hundred feet," he breathed to himself, as the cable markings went by, "three hundred and fifty, four hundred; four hundred and——"

The cable had stopped. Jerry threw off the brake, but it did not move. He caught the cable with his hands and tried to start it by tugging smartly. Something had gone wrong. What? He could not guess; he could not see. Looking up, he could vaguely make out the empty car, which had been crossing from the opposite cliff at a speed equal to that of the loaded car. It was about two hundred and fifty feet away. That meant, he knew, that somewhere in the gray obscurity, two hundred feet above the river and two hundred and fifty feet from the other bank, Spillane and his wife were suspended and stationary.

Three times Jerry shouted with all the shrill force of his lungs, but no answering cry came out of the storm. It was impossible for him to hear them or to make himself heard. As he stood for a moment, thinking rapidly, the flying clouds seemed to thin and lift. He caught a brief glimpse of the swollen Sacramento beneath, and a briefer glimpse of the car and the man and woman. Then the clouds descended thicker than ever.

The boy examined the drum closely, and found nothing the matter with it. Evidently it was the drum on the other side that had gone wrong. He was appalled at the thought of the man and woman out there in the midst of the storm, hanging over the abyss, rocking back and forth in the frail car and ignorant of what was taking place on shore. And he did not like to think of their hanging there while he went round by the Yellow Dragon cable to the other drum.

But he remembered a block and tackle in the tool-house, and ran and brought it. They were double blocks, and he murmured aloud, "A purchase of four," as he made the tackle fast to the endless cable. Then he heaved upon it, heaved until it seemed that his arms were being drawn out from their sockets and that his shoulder muscles would be ripped asunder. Yet the cable did not budge. Nothing remained but to cross over to the other side.

He was already soaking wet, so he did not mind the rain as he ran over the trail to the Yellow Dragon. The storm was with him, and it was easy going, although there was no Hall at the other end of it to man the brake for him and regulate the speed of the car. This he did for himself, however, by means of a stout rope, which he passed, with a turn, round the stationary cable.

As the full force of the wind struck him in mid-air, swaying the cable and whistling and roaring past it, and rocking and careening the car, he appreciated more fully what must be the condition of mind of Spillane and his wife. And this appreciation gave strength to him, as, safely across, he fought his way up the other bank, in the teeth of the gale, to the Yellow Dream cable.

To his consternation, he found the drum in thorough working order. Everything was running smoothly at both ends. Where was the hitch? In the middle, without a doubt.

From this side, the car containing Spillane was only two hundred and fifty feet away. He could make out the man and woman through the whirling vapor, crouching in the bottom of the car and exposed to the pelting rain and the full fury of the wind. In a lull between the squalls he shouted to Spillane to examine the trolley of the car.

Spillane heard, for he saw him rise up cautiously on his knees, and with his hands go over both trolley-wheels. Then he turned his face toward the bank.

"She's all right, kid!"

Jerry heard the words, faint and far, as from a remote distance. Then what was the matter? Nothing remained but the other and empty car, which he could not see, but which he knew to be there, somewhere in that terrible gulf two hundred feet beyond Spillane's car.

His mind was made up on the instant. He was only fourteen years old, slightly and wirily built; but his life had been lived among the mountains, his father had taught him no small measure of "sailoring," and he was not particularly afraid of heights.

In the tool-box by the drum he found an old monkey-wrench and a short bar of iron, also a coil of fairly new Manila rope. He looked in vain for a piece of board with which to rig a "boatswain's chair." There was nothing at hand but large planks, which he had no means of sawing, so he was compelled to do without the more comfortable form of saddle.

The saddle he rigged was very simple. With the rope he made merely a large loop round the stationary cable, to which hung the empty car. When he sat in the loop his hands could just reach the cable conveniently, and where the rope was likely to fray against the cable he lashed his coat, in lieu of the old sack he would have used had he been able to find one.

These preparations swiftly completed, he swung out over the chasm, sitting in the rope saddle and pulling himself along the cable by his hands. With him he carried the monkey-wrench and short iron bar and a few spare feet of rope. It was a slightly up-hill pull, but this he did not mind so much as the wind. When the furious gusts hurled him back and forth, sometimes half twisting him about, and he gazed down into the gray depths, he was aware that he was afraid. It was an old cable. What if it should break under his weight and the pressure of the wind?

It was fear he was experiencing, honest fear, and he knew that there was a "gone" feeling in the pit of his stomach, and a trembling of the knees which he could not quell.

But he held himself bravely to the task. The cable was old and worn, sharp pieces of wire projected from it, and his hands were cut and bleeding by the time he took his first rest, and held a shouted conversation with Spillane. The car was directly beneath him and only a few feet away, so he was able to explain the condition of affairs and his errand.

"Wish I could help you," Spillane shouted at him as he started on, "but the wife's gone all to pieces! Anyway, kid, take care of yourself! I got myself in this fix, but it's up to you to get me out!"

"Oh, I'll do it!" Jerry shouted back. "Tell Mrs. Spillane that she'll be ashore now in a jiffy!"

In the midst of pelting rain, which half-blinded him, swinging from side to side like a rapid and erratic pendulum, his torn hands paining him severely and his lungs panting from his exertions and panting from the very air which the wind sometimes blew into his mouth with strangling force, he finally arrived at the empty car.

A single glance showed him that he had not made the dangerous journey in vain. The front trolley-wheel, loose from long wear, had jumped the cable, and the cable was now jammed tightly between the wheel and the sheave-block.

One thing was clear—the wheel must be removed from the block. A second thing was equally clear—while the wheel was being removed the car would have to be fastened to the cable by the rope he had brought.

At the end of a quarter of an hour, beyond making the car secure, he had accomplished nothing. The key which bound the wheel on its axle was rusted and jammed. He hammered at it with one hand and held on the best he could with the other, but the wind persisted in swinging and twisting his body, and made his blows miss more often than not. Nine-tenths of the strength he expended was in trying to hold himself steady. For fear that he might drop the monkey-wrench he made it fast to his wrist with his handkerchief.

At the end of half an hour Jerry had hammered the key clear, but he could not draw it out. A dozen times it seemed that he must give up in despair, that all the danger and toil he had gone through were for nothing. Then an idea came to him, and he went through his pockets with feverish haste, and found what he sought—a ten-penny nail.

But for that nail, put in his pocket he knew not when or why, he would have had to make another trip over the cable and back. Thrusting the nail through the looped head of the key, he at last had a grip, and in no time the key was out.

Then came punching and prying with the iron bar to get the wheel itself free from where it was jammed by the cable against the side of the block. After that Jerry replaced the wheel, and by means of the rope, heaved up on the car till the trolley once more rested properly on the cable.

All this took time. More than an hour and a half had elapsed since his arrival at the empty car. And now, for the first time, he dropped out of his saddle and down into the car. He removed the detaining ropes, and the trolley-wheel began slowly to revolve. The car was moving, and he knew that somewhere beyond, although he could not see, the car of Spillane was likewise moving, and in the opposite direction.

There was no need for a brake, for his weight sufficiently counterbalanced the weight in the other car; and soon he saw the cliff rising out of the cloud depths and the old familiar drum going round and round.

Jerry climbed out and made the car securely fast. He did it deliberately and carefully, and then, quite unhero-like, he sank down by the drum, regardless of the pelting storm, and burst out sobbing.

There were many reasons why he sobbed—partly from the pain of his hand, which was excruciating; partly from exhaustion; partly from relief and release from the nerve-tension he had been under for so long; and in a large measure for thankfulness that the man and woman were saved.

They were not there to thank him; but somewhere beyond that howling, storm-driven gulf he knew they were hurrying over the trail toward the Clover Leaf.

Jerry staggered to the cabin, and his hand left the white knob red with blood as he opened the door, but he took no notice of it.

He was too proudly contented with himself, for he was certain that he had done well, and he was honest enough to admit to himself that he had done well. But a small regret arose and persisted in his thoughts—if his father had only been there to see!

IN YEDDO BAY

Somewhere along Theater Street he had lost it. He remembered being hustled somewhat roughly on the bridge over one of the canals that cross that busy thoroughfare. Possibly some slant-eyed, light-fingered pickpocket was even then enjoying the fifty-odd yen his purse had contained. And then again, he thought, he might have lost it himself, just lost it carelessly.

Hopelessly, and for the twentieth time, he searched in all his pockets for the missing purse. It was not there. His hand lingered in his empty hip-pocket, and he woefully regarded the voluble and vociferous restaurant-keeper, who insanely clamored: "Twenty-five sen! You pay now! Twenty-five sen!"

"But my purse!" the boy said. "I tell you I've lost it somewhere."

Whereupon the restaurant-keeper lifted his arms indignantly and shrieked: "Twenty-five sen! Twenty-five sen! You pay now!"

Quite a crowd had collected, and it was growing embarrassing for Alf Davis.

It was so ridiculous and petty, Alf thought. Such a disturbance about nothing! And, decidedly, he must be doing something. Thoughts of diving wildly through that forest of legs, and of striking out at whomsoever opposed him, flashed through his mind; but, as though divining his purpose, one of the waiters, a short and chunky chap with an evil-looking cast in one eye, seized him by the arm.

"You pay now! You pay now! Twenty-five sen!" yelled the proprietor, hoarse with rage.

Alf was red in the face, too, from mortification; but he resolutely set out on another exploration. He had given up the purse, pinning his last hope on stray coins. In the little change-pocket of his coat he found a ten-sen piece and five-copper sen; and remembering having recently missed a ten-sen piece, he cut the seam of the pocket and resurrected the coin from the depths of the lining. Twenty-five sen he held in his hand, the sum required to pay for the supper he had eaten. He turned them over to the proprietor, who counted them, grew suddenly calm, and bowed obsequiously—in fact, the whole crowd bowed obsequiously and melted away.

Alf Davis was a young sailor, just turned sixteen, on board the *Annie Mine*, an American sailing-schooner, which had run into Yokohama to ship its season's catch of skins to London. And in this, his second trip ashore, he was beginning to snatch his first puzzling glimpses of the Oriental mind. He laughed when the bowing and kotowing was over, and turned on his heel to confront another problem. How was he to get aboard ship? It was eleven o'clock at night, and there would be no ship's boats ashore, while the outlook for hiring a native boatman, with nothing but empty pockets to draw upon, was not particularly inviting.

Keeping a sharp lookout for shipmates, he went down to the pier. At Yokohama there are no long lines of wharves. The shipping lies out at anchor, enabling a few hundred of the short-legged people to make a livelihood by carrying passengers to and from the shore.

A dozen sampan men and boys hailed Alf and offered their services. He selected the most favorable-looking one, an old and beneficent-appearing man with a withered leg. Alf stepped into his sampan and sat down. It was quite dark and he could not see what the old fellow was doing, though he evidently was doing nothing about shoving off and getting under way. At last he limped over and peered into Alf's face.

"Ten sen," he said.

"Yes, I know, ten sen," Alf answered carelessly. "But hurry up. American schooner."

"Ten sen. You pay now," the old fellow insisted.

Alf felt himself grow hot all over at the hateful words "pay now." "You take me to American schooner; then I pay," he said.

But the man stood up patiently before him, held out his hand, and said, "Ten sen. You pay now."

Alf tried to explain. He had no money. He had lost his purse. But he would pay. As soon as he got aboard the American schooner, then he would pay. No; he would not even go aboard the American schooner. He would call to his shipmates, and they would give the sampan man the ten sen first. After that he would go aboard. So it was all right, of course.

To all of which the beneficent-appearing old man replied: "You pay now. Ten sen." And, to make matters worse, the other sampan men squatted on the pier steps, listening.

Alf, chagrined and angry, stood up to step ashore. But the old fellow laid a detaining hand on his sleeve. "You give shirt now. I take you 'Merican schooner," he proposed.

Then it was that all of Alf's American independence flamed up in his breast. The Anglo-Saxon has a born dislike of being imposed upon, and to Alf this was sheer robbery! Ten sen was equivalent to six American cents, while his shirt, which was of good quality and was new, had cost him two dollars.

He turned his back on the man without a word, and went out to the end of the pier, the crowd, laughing with great gusto, following at his heels. The majority of them were heavy-set, muscular fellows, and the July night being one of sweltering heat, they were clad in the least possible raiment. The water-people of any race are rough and turbulent, and it struck Alf that to be out at midnight on a pier-end with such a crowd of wharfmen, in a big Japanese city, was not as safe as it might be.

One burly fellow, with a shock of black hair and ferocious eyes, came up. The rest shoved in after him to take part in the discussion.

"Give me shoes," the man said. "Give me shoes now. I take you 'Merican schooner."

Alf shook his head, whereat the crowd clamored that he accept the proposal. Now the Anglo-Saxon is so constituted that to browbeat or bully him is the last way under the sun of getting him to do any certain thing. He will dare willingly, but he will not permit himself to be driven. So this attempt of the boatmen to force Alf only aroused all the dogged stubbornness of his race. The same qualities were in him that are in men who lead forlorn hopes; and there, under the stars, on the lonely pier, encircled by the jostling and shouldering gang, he resolved that he would die rather than submit to the indignity of being robbed of a single stitch of clothing. Not value, but principle, was at stake.

Then somebody thrust roughly against him from behind. He whirled about with flashing eyes, and the circle involuntarily gave ground. But the crowd was growing more boisterous. Each and every article of clothing he had on was demanded by one or another, and these demands were shouted simultaneously at the tops of very healthy lungs.

Alf had long since ceased to say anything, but he knew that the situation was getting dangerous, and that the only thing left to him was to get away. His face was set doggedly, his eyes glinted like points of steel, and his body was firmly and confidently poised. This air of determination sufficiently impressed the boatmen to make them give way before him When he started to walk toward the shore-end of the pier. But they trooped along beside more noisily than ever. One of the youngsters about Alf's size and build, impudently snatched his cap from his head; and before he could put it on his own head, Alf struck out from the shoulder, and sent the fellow rolling on the stones.

The cap flew out of his hand and disappeared among the many legs. Alf did some quick thinking, his sailor pride would not permit him to leave the cap in their hands. He followed in the direction it had sped, and soon found it under the bare foot of a stalwart fellow, who kept his weight stolidly upon it. Alf tried to get the cap by a sudden jerk, but failed. He shoved against the man's leg, but the man only grunted. It was challenge direct, and Alf accepted it. Like a flash one leg was behind the man and Alf had thrust strongly with his shoulder against the fellow's chest. Nothing could save the man from the fierce vigorousness of the trick, and he was hurled over and backward.

Next, the cap was on Alf's head and his fists were up before him. Then he whirled about to prevent attack from behind, and all those in that quarter fled precipitately. This was what he wanted. None remained between him and the shore end. The pier was narrow. Facing them and threatening with his fist those who attempted to pass him on either side, he continued his retreat. It was exciting work, walking backward and at the same time checking that surging mass of men. But the dark-skinned peoples, the world over, have learned to respect the white man's fist; and it was the battles fought by many sailors, more than his own warlike front, that gave Alf the victory.

Where the pier adjoins the shore was the station of the harbor police, and Alf backed into the electric-lighted office, very much to the amusement of the dapper lieutenant in charge. The sampan men, grown quiet and orderly, clustered like flies by the open door, through which they could see and hear what passed.

Alf explained his difficulty in few words, and demanded, as the privilege of a stranger in a strange land, that the lieutenant put him aboard in the police-boat. The lieutenant, in turn, who knew all the "rules and regulations" by heart, explained that the harbor police were not ferrymen, and that the police-boats had other functions to perform than that of transporting belated and penniless sailormen to their ships. He also said he knew the sampan men to be natural-born robbers, but that so long as they robbed within the law he was powerless. It was their right to collect fares in advance, and who was he to command them to take a passenger and collect fare at the journey's end? Alf acknowledged the justice of his remarks, but suggested that while he could not command he might persuade. The lieutenant was willing to oblige, and went to the door, from where he delivered a speech to the crowd. But they, too, knew their rights, and, when the officer had finished, shouted in chorus their abominable "Ten sen! You pay now! You pay now!"

"You see, I can do nothing," said the lieutenant, who, by the way, spoke perfect English. "But I have warned them not to harm or molest you, so you will be safe, at least. The night is warm and half over. Lie down somewhere and go to sleep. I would permit you to sleep here in the office, were it not against the rules and regulations."

Alf thanked him for his kindness and courtesy; but the sampan men had aroused all his pride of race and doggedness, and the problem could not be solved that way. To sleep out the night on the stones was an acknowledgment of defeat.

"The sampan men refuse to take me out?"

The lieutenant nodded.

"And you refuse to take me out?"

Again the lieutenant nodded.

"Well, then, it's not in the rules and regulations that you can prevent my taking myself out?"

The lieutenant was perplexed. "There is no boat," he said.

"That's not the question," Alf proclaimed hotly. "If I take myself out, everybody's satisfied and no harm done?"

"Yes; what you say is true," persisted the puzzled lieutenant. "But you cannot take yourself out."

"You just watch me," was the retort.

Down went Alf's cap on the office floor. Right and left he kicked off his low-cut shoes. Trousers and shirt followed.

"Remember," he said in ringing tones, "I, as a citizen of the United States, shall hold you, the city of Yokohama, and the government of Japan responsible for those clothes. Good night."

He plunged through the doorway, scattering the astounded boatmen to either side, and ran out on the pier. But they quickly recovered and ran after him, shouting with glee at the new phase the situation had taken on. It was a night long remembered among the water-folk of Yokohama town. Straight to the end Alf ran, and, without pause, dived off cleanly and neatly into the water. He struck out with a lusty, single-overhand stroke till curiosity prompted him to halt for a moment. Out of the darkness, from where the pier should be, voices were calling to him.

He turned on his back, floated, and listened.

"All right! All right!" he could distinguish from the babel. "No pay now; pay bime by! Come back! Come back now; pay bime by!"

"No, thank you," he called back. "No pay at all. Good night."

Then he faced about in order to locate the *Annie Mine*. She was fully a mile away, and in the darkness it was no easy task to get her bearings. First, he settled upon a blaze of lights which he knew nothing but a man-of-war could make. That must be the United States war-ship *Lancaster*. Somewhere to the left and beyond should be the *Annie Mine*. But to the left he made out three lights close together. That could not be the schooner. For the moment he was confused. He rolled over on his back and shut his eyes, striving to construct a mental picture of the harbor as he had seen it in daytime. With a snort of satisfaction he rolled back again. The three lights evidently belonged to the big English tramp steamer. Therefore the schooner must lie somewhere between the three lights and the *Lancaster*. He gazed long and steadily, and there, very dim and low, but at the point he expected, burned a single light—the anchor-light of the *Annie Mine*.

And it was a fine swim under the starshine. The air was warm as the water, and the water as warm as tepid milk. The good salt taste of it was in his mouth, the tingling of it along his limbs; and the steady beat of his heart, heavy and strong, made him glad for living.

But beyond being glorious the swim was uneventful. On the right hand he passed the many-lighted *Lancaster*, on the left hand the English tramp, and ere long the *Annie Mine* loomed large above him. He grasped the hanging rope-ladder and drew himself noiselessly on deck. There was no one in sight. He saw a light in the galley, and knew that the captain's son, who kept the lonely anchor-watch, was making coffee. Alf went forward to the forecastle. The men were snoring in their bunks, and in that confined space the heat seemed to him insufferable. So he put on a thin cotton shirt and a pair of dungaree trousers, tucked blanket and pillow under his arm, and went up on deck and out on the forecastle-head.

Hardly had he begun to doze when he was roused by a boat coming alongside and hailing the anchor-watch. It was the police-boat, and to Alf it was given to enjoy the excited conversation that ensued. Yes, the captain's son recognized the clothes. They belonged to Alf Davis, one of the seamen.

What had happened? No; Alf Davis had not come aboard. He was ashore. He was not ashore? Then he must be drowned. Here both the lieutenant and the captain's son talked at the same time, and Alf could make out nothing. Then he heard them come forward and rouse out the crew. The crew grumbled sleepily and said that Alf Davis was not in the forecastle; whereupon the captain's son waxed indignant at the Yokohama police and their ways, and the lieutenant quoted rules and regulations in despairing accents.

Alf rose up from the forecastle-head and extended his hand, saying:

"I guess I'll take those clothes. Thank you for bringing them aboard so promptly."

"I don't see why he couldn't have brought you aboard inside of them," said the captain's son.

And the police lieutenant said nothing, though he turned the clothes over somewhat sheepishly to their rightful owner.

The next day, when Alf started to go ashore, he found himself surrounded by shouting and gesticulating, though very respectful, sampan men, all extraordinarily anxious to have him for a passenger. Nor did the one he selected say, "You pay now," when he entered his boat. When Alf prepared to step out on to the pier, he offered the man the customary ten sen. But the man drew himself up and shook his head.

"You all right," he said. "You no pay. You never no pay. You bully boy and all right."

And for the rest of the *Annie Mine*'s stay in port, the sampan men refused money at Alf Davis's hand. Out of admiration for his pluck and independence, they had given him the freedom of the harbor.

About Author

John Griffith London (born **John Griffith Chaney**; January 12, 1876 – November 22, 1916) was an American novelist, journalist, and social activist. A pioneer in the world of commercial magazine fiction, he was one of the first writers to become a worldwide celebrity and earn a large fortune from writing. He was also an innovator in the genre that would later become known as science fiction.

His most famous works include The Call of the Wild and White Fang, both set in the Klondike Gold Rush, as well as the short stories "To Build a Fire", "An Odyssey of the North", and "Love of Life". He also wrote about the South Pacific in stories such as "The Pearls of Parlay", and "The Heathen".

London was part of the radical literary group "The Crowd" in San Francisco and a passionate advocate of unionization, workers' rights, socialism, and eugenics. He wrote several works dealing with these topics, such as his dystopian novel The Iron Heel, his non-fiction exposé The People of the Abyss, The War of the Classes, and Before Adam.

Family

Jack London's mother, Flora Wellman, was the fifth and youngest child of Pennsylvania Canal builder Marshall Wellman and his first wife, Eleanor Garrett Jones. Marshall Wellman was descended from Thomas Wellman, an early Puritan settler in the Massachusetts Bay Colony. Flora left Ohio and moved to the Pacific coast when her father remarried after her mother died. In San Francisco, Flora worked as a music teacher and spiritualist, claiming to channel the spirit of a Sauk chief, Black Hawk.

Biographer Clarice Stasz and others believe London's father was astrologer William Chaney. Flora Wellman was living with Chaney in San Francisco when she became pregnant. Whether Wellman and Chaney were legally married is unknown. Stasz notes that in his memoirs, Chaney refers to London's mother Flora Wellman as having been his "wife"; he also cites an advertisement in which Flora called herself "Florence Wellman Chaney".

According to Flora Wellman's account, as recorded in the San Francisco Chronicle of June 4, 1875, Chaney demanded that she have an abortion. When she refused, he disclaimed responsibility for the child. In desperation, she shot herself. She was not seriously wounded, but she was temporarily deranged. After giving birth, Flora turned the baby over for care to Virginia Prentiss, an African-American woman and former slave. She was a major maternal figure throughout London's life. Late in 1876, Flora Wellman married John London, a partially disabled Civil War veteran, and brought her baby John, later known as Jack, to live with the newly married couple. The family moved around the San Francisco Bay Area before settling in Oakland, where London completed public grade school.

In 1897, when he was 21 and a student at the University of California, Berkeley, London searched for and read the newspaper accounts of his mother's suicide attempt and the name of his biological father. He wrote to William Chaney, then living in Chicago. Chaney responded that he could not be London's father because he was impotent; he casually asserted that London's mother had relations with other men and averred that she had slandered him when she said he insisted on an abortion. Chaney concluded by saying that he was more to be pitied than London. London was devastated by his father's letter; in the months following, he quit school at Berkeley and went to the Klondike during the gold rush boom.

Early life

London was born near Third and Brannan Streets in San Francisco. The house burned down in the fire after the 1906 San Francisco earthquake; the California Historical Society placed a plaque at the site in 1953. Although the family was working class, it was not as impoverished as London's later accounts claimed. London was largely self-educated.

In 1885, London found and read Ouida's long Victorian novel Signa. He credited this as the seed of his literary success. In 1886, he went to the Oakland Public Library and found a sympathetic librarian, Ina Coolbrith, who encouraged his learning. (She later became California's first poet laureate and an important figure in the San Francisco literary community).

In 1889, London began working 12 to 18 hours a day at Hickmott's Cannery. Seeking a way out, he borrowed money from his foster mother Virginia Prentiss, bought the sloop Razzle-Dazzle from an oyster pirate named French Frank, and became an oyster pirate himself. In his memoir, John Barleycorn, he claims also to have stolen French Frank's mistress Mamie. After a few months, his sloop became damaged beyond repair. London hired on as a member of the California Fish Patrol.

In 1893, he signed on to the sealing schooner Sophie Sutherland, bound for the coast of Japan. When he returned, the country was in the grip of the panic of '93 and Oakland was swept by labor unrest. After grueling jobs in a jute mill and a street-railway power plant, London joined Coxey's Army and began his career as a tramp. In 1894, he spent 30 days for vagrancy in the Erie County Penitentiary at Buffalo, New York. In The Road, he wrote:

> Man-handling was merely one of the very minor unprintable horrors of the Erie County Pen. I say 'unprintable'; and in justice I must also say undescribable. They were unthinkable to me until I saw them, and I was no spring chicken in the ways of the world and the awful abysses of human degradation. It would take a deep plummet to reach bottom in the Erie County Pen, and I do but skim lightly and facetiously the surface of things as I there saw them.

> —Jack London, The Road

After many experiences as a hobo and a sailor, he returned to Oakland and attended Oakland High School. He contributed a number of articles to the high school's magazine, The Aegis. His first published work was "Typhoon off the Coast of Japan", an account of his sailing experiences.

As a schoolboy, London often studied at Heinold's First and Last Chance Saloon, a port-side bar in Oakland. At 17, he confessed to the bar's owner, John Heinold, his desire to attend university and pursue a career as a writer. Heinold lent London tuition money to attend college.

London desperately wanted to attend the University of California, located in Berkeley. In 1896, after a summer of intense studying to pass certification exams, he was admitted. Financial circumstances forced him to leave in 1897 and he never graduated. No evidence has surfaced that he ever wrote for student publications while studying at Berkeley.

While at Berkeley, London continued to study and spend time at Heinold's saloon, where he was introduced to the sailors and adventurers who would influence his writing. In his autobiographical novel, John Barleycorn, London mentioned the pub's likeness seventeen times. Heinold's was the place where London met Alexander McLean, a captain known for his cruelty at sea. London based his protagonist Wolf Larsen, in the novel The Sea-Wolf, on McLean.

Heinold's First and Last Chance Saloon is now unofficially named Jack London's Rendezvous in his honor.

Gold rush and first success

On July 12, 1897, London (age 21) and his sister's husband Captain Shepard sailed to join the Klondike Gold Rush. This was the setting for some of his first successful stories. London's time in the harsh Klondike, however, was detrimental to his health. Like so many other men who were malnourished in the goldfields, London developed scurvy. His gums became swollen, leading to the loss of his four front teeth. A constant gnawing pain affected his hip and leg muscles, and his face was stricken with marks that always reminded him of the struggles he faced in the Klondike. Father William Judge, "The Saint of Dawson", had a facility in Dawson that provided shelter, food and any available medicine to London and others. His struggles there inspired London's short story, "To Build a Fire" (1902, revised in 1908), which many critics assess as his best.

His landlords in Dawson were mining engineers Marshall Latham Bond and Louis Whitford Bond, educated at Yale and Stanford, respectively. The brothers' father, Judge Hiram Bond, was a wealthy mining investor. The Bonds, especially Hiram, were active Republicans. Marshall Bond's diary mentions friendly sparring with London on political issues as a camp pastime.

136

London left Oakland with a social conscience and socialist leanings; he returned to become an activist for socialism. He concluded that his only hope of escaping the work "trap" was to get an education and "sell his brains". He saw his writing as a business, his ticket out of poverty, and, he hoped, a means of beating the wealthy at their own game. On returning to California in 1898, London began working to get published, a struggle described in his novel, Martin Eden (serialized in 1908, published in 1909). His first published story since high school was "To the Man On Trail", which has frequently been collected in anthologies. When The Overland Monthly offered him only five dollars for it—and was slow paying—London came close to abandoning his writing career. In his words, "literally and literarily I was saved" when The Black Cat accepted his story "A Thousand Deaths", and paid him $40—the "first money I ever received for a story".

London began his writing career just as new printing technologies enabled lower-cost production of magazines. This resulted in a boom in popular magazines aimed at a wide public audience and a strong market for short fiction. In 1900, he made $2,500 in writing, about $77,000 in today's currency. Among the works he sold to magazines was a short story known as either "Diable" (1902) or "Bâtard" (1904), two editions of the same basic story; London received $141.25 for this story on May 27, 1902. In the text, a cruel French Canadian brutalizes his dog, and the dog retaliates and kills the man. London told some of his critics that man's actions are the main cause of the behavior of their animals, and he would show this in another story, The Call of the Wild.

In early 1903, London sold The Call of the Wild to The Saturday Evening Post for $750, and the book rights to Macmillan for $2,000. Macmillan's promotional campaign propelled it to swift success.

While living at his rented villa on Lake Merritt in Oakland, California, London met poet George Sterling; in time they became best friends. In 1902, Sterling helped London find a home closer to his own in nearby Piedmont. In his letters London addressed Sterling as "Greek", owing to Sterling's aquiline nose and classical profile, and he signed them as "Wolf". London was later to depict Sterling as Russ Brissenden in his autobiographical novel Martin Eden (1910) and as Mark Hall in The Valley of the Moon (1913).

In later life London indulged his wide-ranging interests by accumulating a personal library of 15,000 volumes. He referred to his books as "the tools of my trade".

First marriage (1900–04)

London married Elizabeth "Bessie" Maddern on April 7, 1900, the same day The Son of the Wolf was published. Bess had been part of his circle of friends for a number of years. She was related to stage actresses Minnie Maddern Fiske and Emily Stevens. Stasz says, "Both acknowledged publicly that they were not marrying out of love, but from friendship and a belief that they would produce sturdy children." Kingman says, "they were comfortable together... Jack had made it clear to Bessie that he did not love her, but that he liked her enough to make a successful marriage."

London met Bessie through his friend at Oakland High School, Fred Jacobs; she was Fred's fiancée. Bessie, who tutored at Anderson's University Academy in Alameda California, tutored Jack in preparation for his entrance exams for the University of California at Berkeley in 1896. Jacobs was killed aboard the USAT Scandia in 1897, but Jack and Bessie continued their friendship, which included taking photos and developing the film together. This was the beginning of Jack's passion for photography.

During the marriage, London continued his friendship with Anna Strunsky, co-authoring The Kempton-Wace Letters, an epistolary novel contrasting two philosophies of love. Anna, writing "Dane Kempton's" letters, arguing for a romantic view of marriage, while London, writing "Herbert Wace's" letters, argued for a scientific view, based on Darwinism and eugenics. In the novel, his fictional character contrasted two women he had known.

London's pet name for Bess was "Mother-Girl" and Bess's for London was "Daddy-Boy". Their first child, Joan, was born on January 15, 1901, and their second, Bessie (later called Becky), on October 20, 1902. Both children were born in Piedmont, California. Here London wrote one of his most celebrated works, The Call of the Wild.

138

While London had pride in his children, the marriage was strained. Kingman says that by 1903 the couple were close to separation as they were "extremely incompatible". "Jack was still so kind and gentle with Bessie that when Cloudsley Johns was a house guest in February 1903 he didn't suspect a breakup of their marriage."

London reportedly complained to friends Joseph Noel and George Sterling:

> [Bessie] is devoted to purity. When I tell her morality is only evidence of low blood pressure, she hates me. She'd sell me and the children out for her damned purity. It's terrible. Every time I come back after being away from home for a night she won't let me be in the same room with her if she can help it.

Stasz writes that these were "code words for fear that was consorting with prostitutes and might bring home venereal disease."

On July 24, 1903, London told Bessie he was leaving and moved out. During 1904, London and Bess negotiated the terms of a divorce, and the decree was granted on November 11, 1904.

War correspondent (1904)

London accepted an assignment of the San Francisco Examiner to cover the Russo-Japanese War in early 1904, arriving in Yokohama on January 25, 1904. He was arrested by Japanese authorities in Shimonoseki, but released through the intervention of American ambassador Lloyd Griscom. After travelling to Korea, he was again arrested by Japanese authorities for straying too close to the border with Manchuria without official permission, and was sent back to Seoul. Released again, London was permitted to travel with the Imperial Japanese Army to the border, and to observe the Battle of the Yalu.

London asked William Randolph Hearst, the owner of the San Francisco Examiner, to be allowed to transfer to the Imperial Russian Army, where he felt that restrictions on his reporting and his movements would be less severe. However, before this could be arranged, he was arrested for a third time in four months, this time for assaulting his Japanese assistants, whom he accused of stealing the fodder for his horse. Released through the personal intervention of President Theodore Roosevelt, London departed the front in June 1904.

Bohemian Club

On August 18, 1904, London went with his close friend, the poet George Sterling, to "Summer High Jinks" at the Bohemian Grove. London was elected to honorary membership in the Bohemian Club and took part in many activities. Other noted members of the Bohemian Club during this time included Ambrose Bierce, Gelett Burgess, Allan Dunn, John Muir, Frank Norris, and Herman George Scheffauer.

Beginning in December 1914, London worked on The Acorn Planter, A California Forest Play, to be performed as one of the annual Grove Plays, but it was never selected. It was described as too difficult to set to music. London published The Acorn Planter in 1916.

Second marriage

After divorcing Maddern, London married Charmian Kittredge in 1905. London had been introduced to Kittredge in 1900 by her aunt Netta Eames, who was an editor at Overland Monthly magazine in San Francisco. The two met prior to his first marriage but became lovers years later after Jack and Bessie London visited Wake Robin, Netta Eames' Sonoma County resort, in 1903. London was injured when he fell from a buggy, and Netta arranged for Charmian to care for him. The two developed a friendship, as Charmian, Netta, her husband Roscoe, and London were politically aligned with socialist causes. At some point the relationship became romantic, and Jack divorced his wife to marry Charmian, who was five years his senior.

Biographer Russ Kingman called Charmian "Jack's soul-mate, always at his side, and a perfect match." Their time together included numerous trips, including a 1907 cruise on the yacht Snark to Hawaii and Australia. Many of London's stories are based on his visits to Hawaii, the last one for 10 months beginning in December 1915.

140

The couple also visited Goldfield, Nevada, in 1907, where they were guests of the Bond brothers, London's Dawson City landlords. The Bond brothers were working in Nevada as mining engineers.

London had contrasted the concepts of the "Mother Girl" and the "Mate Woman" in The Kempton-Wace Letters. His pet name for Bess had been "Mother-Girl;" his pet name for Charmian was "Mate-Woman." Charmian's aunt and foster mother, a disciple of Victoria Woodhull, had raised her without prudishness. Every biographer alludes to Charmian's uninhibited sexuality.

Joseph Noel calls the events from 1903 to 1905 "a domestic drama that would have intrigued the pen of an Ibsen.... London's had comedy relief in it and a sort of easy-going romance." In broad outline, London was restless in his first marriage, sought extramarital sexual affairs, and found, in Charmian Kittredge, not only a sexually active and adventurous partner, but his future life-companion. They attempted to have children; one child died at birth, and another pregnancy ended in a miscarriage.

In 1906, London published in Collier's magazine his eye-witness report of the San Francisco earthquake.

Beauty Ranch (1905–16)

In 1905, London purchased a 1,000 acres (4.0 km2) ranch in Glen Ellen, Sonoma County, California, on the eastern slope of Sonoma Mountain. He wrote: "Next to my wife, the ranch is the dearest thing in the world to me." He desperately wanted the ranch to become a successful business enterprise. Writing, always a commercial enterprise with London, now became even more a means to an end: "I write for no other purpose than to add to the beauty that now belongs to me. I write a book for no other reason than to add three or four hundred acres to my magnificent estate."

Stasz writes that London "had taken fully to heart the vision, expressed in his agrarian fiction, of the land as the closest earthly version of Eden ... he educated himself through the study of agricultural manuals and scientific tomes. He conceived of a system of ranching that today would be praised

141

for its ecological wisdom." He was proud to own the first concrete silo in California, a circular piggery that he designed. He hoped to adapt the wisdom of Asian sustainable agriculture to the United States. He hired both Italian and Chinese stonemasons, whose distinctly different styles are obvious.

The ranch was an economic failure. Sympathetic observers such as Stasz treat his projects as potentially feasible, and ascribe their failure to bad luck or to being ahead of their time. Unsympathetic historians such as Kevin Starr suggest that he was a bad manager, distracted by other concerns and impaired by his alcoholism. Starr notes that London was absent from his ranch about six months a year between 1910 and 1916 and says, "He liked the show of managerial power, but not grinding attention to detail .... London's workers laughed at his efforts to play big-time rancher the operation a rich man's hobby."

London spent $80,000 ($2,280,000 in current value) to build a 15,000-square-foot (1,400 m2) stone mansion called Wolf House on the property. Just as the mansion was nearing completion, two weeks before the Londons planned to move in, it was destroyed by fire.

London's last visit to Hawaii, beginning in December 1915, lasted eight months. He met with Duke Kahanamoku, Prince Jonah Kūhiō Kalaniana'ole, Queen Lili'uokalani and many others, before returning to his ranch in July 1916. He was suffering from kidney failure, but he continued to work.

The ranch (abutting stone remnants of Wolf House) is now a National Historic Landmark and is protected in Jack London State Historic Park.

Animal activism

London witnessed animal cruelty in the training of circus animals, and his subsequent novels Jerry of the Islands and Michael, Brother of Jerry included a foreword entreating the public to become more informed about this practice. In 1918, the Massachusetts Society for the Prevention of Cruelty to Animals and the American Humane Education Society teamed up to create the Jack London Club, which sought to inform the public about cruelty to circus animals and encourage them to protest this establishment. Support from Club members led to a temporary cessation of trained animal acts at Ringling-Barnum and Bailey in 1925.

Death

London died November 22, 1916, in a sleeping porch in a cottage on his ranch. London had been a robust man but had suffered several serious illnesses, including scurvy in the Klondike. Additionally, during travels on the Snark, he and Charmian picked up unspecified tropical infections, and diseases, including yaws. At the time of his death, he suffered from dysentery, late-stage alcoholism, and uremia; he was in extreme pain and taking morphine.

London's ashes were buried on his property not far from the Wolf House. London's funeral took place on November 26, 1916, attended only by close friends, relatives, and workers of the property. In accordance with his wishes, he was cremated and buried next to some pioneer children, under a rock that belonged to the Wolf House. After Charmian's death in 1955, she was also cremated and then buried with her husband in the same spot that her husband chose. The grave is marked by a mossy boulder. The buildings and property were later preserved as Jack London State Historic Park, in Glen Ellen, California.

Suicide debate

Because he was using morphine, many older sources describe London's death as a suicide, and some still do. This conjecture appears to be a rumor, or speculation based on incidents in his fiction writings. His death certificate gives the cause as uremia, following acute renal colic.

The biographer Stasz writes, "Following London's death, for a number of reasons, a biographical myth developed in which he has been portrayed as an alcoholic womanizer who committed suicide. Recent scholarship based upon firsthand documents challenges this caricature." Most biographers, including Russ Kingman, now agree he died of uremia aggravated by an accidental morphine overdose.

London's fiction featured several suicides. In his autobiographical memoir John Barleycorn, he claims, as a youth, to have drunkenly stumbled overboard into the San Francisco Bay, "some maundering fancy of going out with the tide suddenly obsessed me". He said he drifted and nearly succeeded in drowning before sobering up and being rescued by fishermen. In the dénouement of The Little Lady of the Big House, the heroine, confronted by the pain of a mortal gunshot wound, undergoes a physician-assisted suicide by morphine. Also, in Martin Eden, the principal protagonist, who shares certain characteristics with London, drowns himself.

Plagiarism accusations

London was vulnerable to accusations of plagiarism, both because he was such a conspicuous, prolific, and successful writer and because of his methods of working. He wrote in a letter to Elwyn Hoffman, "expression, you see—with me—is far easier than invention." He purchased plots and novels from the young Sinclair Lewis and used incidents from newspaper clippings as writing material.

In July 1901, two pieces of fiction appeared within the same month: London's "Moon-Face", in the San Francisco Argonaut, and Frank Norris' "The Passing of Cock-eye Blacklock", in Century Magazine. Newspapers showed the similarities between the stories, which London said were "quite different in manner of treatment, patently the same in foundation and motive." London explained both writers based their stories on the same newspaper account. A year later, it was discovered that Charles Forrest McLean had published a fictional story also based on the same incident.

Egerton Ryerson Young claimed The Call of the Wild (1903) was taken from Young's book My Dogs in the Northland (1902). London acknowledged using it as a source and claimed to have written a letter to Young thanking him.

In 1906, the New York World published "deadly parallel" columns showing eighteen passages from London's short story "Love of Life" side by side with similar passages from a nonfiction article by Augustus Biddle and J. K. Macdonald, titled "Lost in the Land of the Midnight Sun". London noted the World did not accuse him of "plagiarism", but only of "identity of time and situation", to which he defiantly "pled guilty".

The most serious charge of plagiarism was based on London's "The Bishop's Vision", Chapter 7 of his novel The Iron Heel (1908). The chapter is nearly identical to an ironic essay that Frank Harris published in 1901, titled "The Bishop of London and Public Morality". Harris was incensed and suggested he should receive 1/60th of the royalties from The Iron Heel, the disputed material constituting about that fraction of the whole novel. London insisted he had clipped a reprint of the article, which had appeared in an American newspaper, and believed it to be a genuine speech delivered by the Bishop of London.

Views

Atheism

London was an atheist. He is quoted as saying, "I believe that when I am dead, I am dead. I believe that with my death I am just as much obliterated as the last mosquito you and I squashed."

Socialism

London wrote from a socialist viewpoint, which is evident in his novel The Iron Heel. Neither a theorist nor an intellectual socialist, London's socialism grew out of his life experience. As London explained in his essay, "How I Became a Socialist", his views were influenced by his experience with people at the bottom of the social pit. His optimism and individualism faded, and he vowed never to do more hard physical work than necessary. He wrote that his individualism was hammered out of him, and he was politically reborn. He often closed his letters "Yours for the Revolution."

London joined the Socialist Labor Party in April 1896. In the same year, the San Francisco Chronicle published a story about the twenty-year-old London's giving nightly speeches in Oakland's City Hall Park, an activity he was arrested for a year later. In 1901, he left the Socialist Labor Party and joined the new Socialist Party of America. He ran unsuccessfully as the high-profile Socialist candidate for mayor of Oakland in 1901 (receiving 245 votes) and 1905 (improving to 981 votes), toured the country lecturing on socialism in 1906, and published two collections of essays about socialism: The War of the Classes (1905) and Revolution, and other Essays (1906).

Stasz notes that "London regarded the Wobblies as a welcome addition to the Socialist cause, although he never joined them in going so far as to recommend sabotage." Stasz mentions a personal meeting between London and Big Bill Haywood in 1912.

In his late (1913) book The Cruise of the Snark, London writes about appeals to him for membership of the Snark's crew from office workers and other "toilers" who longed for escape from the cities, and of being cheated by workmen.

In his Glen Ellen ranch years, London felt some ambivalence toward socialism and complained about the "inefficient Italian labourers" in his employ. In 1916, he resigned from the Glen Ellen chapter of the Socialist Party, but stated emphatically he did so "because of its lack of fire and fight, and its loss of emphasis on the class struggle." In an unflattering portrait of London's ranch days, California cultural historian Kevin Starr refers to this period as "post-socialist" and says "... by 1911 ... London was more bored by the class struggle than he cared to admit."

Race

London shared common concerns among many European Americans in California about Asian immigration, described as "the yellow peril"; he used the latter term as the title of a 1904 essay. This theme was also the subject of a story he wrote in 1910 called "The Unparalleled Invasion". Presented as an historical essay set in the future, the story narrates events between 1976 and 1987, in which China, with an ever-increasing population, is taking over and colonizing its neighbors with the intention of taking over the entire Earth. The western nations respond with biological warfare and bombard China with dozens of the most infectious diseases. On his fears about China, he admits, "it must be taken into consideration that the above postulate is itself a product of Western race-egotism, urged by our belief in our own righteousness and fostered by a faith in ourselves which may be as erroneous as are most fond race fancies."

146

By contrast, many of London's short stories are notable for their empathetic portrayal of Mexican ("The Mexican"), Asian ("The Chinago"), and Hawaiian ("Koolau the Leper") characters. London's war correspondence from the Russo-Japanese War, as well as his unfinished novel Cherry, show he admired much about Japanese customs and capabilities. London's writings have been popular among the Japanese, who believe he portrayed them positively.

In "Koolau the Leper", London describes Koolau, who is a Hawaiian leper—and thus a very different sort of "superman" than Martin Eden—and who fights off an entire cavalry troop to elude capture, as "indomitable spiritually—a ... magnificent rebel". This character is based on Hawaiian leper Kaluaikoolau, who in 1893 revolted and resisted capture from forces of the Provisional Government of Hawaii in the Kalalau Valley.

An amateur boxer and avid boxing fan, London reported on the 1910 Johnson–Jeffries fight, in which the black boxer Jack Johnson vanquished Jim Jeffries, known as the "Great White Hope". In 1908, London had reported on an earlier fight of Johnson's, contrasting the black boxer's coolness and intellectual style, with the apelike appearance and fighting style of his Canadian opponent, Tommy Burns:

> [What won] on Saturday was bigness, coolness, quickness, cleverness, and vast physical superiority ... Because a white man wishes a white man to win, this should not prevent him from giving absolute credit to the best man, even when that best man was black. All hail to Johnson. ... superb. He was impregnable ... as inaccessible as Mont Blanc.

Those who defend London against charges of racism cite the letter he wrote to the Japanese-American Commercial Weekly in 1913:

> In reply to yours of August 16, 1913. First of all, I should say by stopping the stupid newspaper from always fomenting race prejudice. This of course, being impossible, I would say, next, by educating the people of Japan so that they will be too intelligently tolerant to respond to any call to race prejudice. And, finally, by realizing, in industry and

government, of socialism—which last word is merely a word that stands for the actual application of in the affairs of men of the theory of the Brotherhood of Man.

In the meantime the nations and races are only unruly boys who have not yet grown to the stature of men. So we must expect them to do unruly and boisterous things at times. And, just as boys grow up, so the races of mankind will grow up and laugh when they look back upon their childish quarrels.

In 1996, after the City of Whitehorse, Yukon, renamed a street in honor of London, protests over London's alleged racism forced the city to change the name of "Jack London Boulevard"[failed verification] back to "Two-mile Hill".

Eugenics

London supported eugenics, including forced sterilization of criminals or those deemed feeble minded. His novel Before Adam(1906–07) has been described as having pro-eugenic themes.

London wrote to Frederick H. Robinson of the periodical Medical Review of Reviews, stating, "I believe the future belongs to eugenics, and will be determined by the practice of eugenics."

Works

Short stories

Western writer and historian Dale L. Walker writes:

London's true métier was the short story ... London's true genius lay in the short form, 7,500 words and under, where the flood of images in his teeming brain and the innate power of his narrative gift were at once constrained and freed. His stories that run longer than the magic 7,500 generally—but certainly not always—could have benefited from self-editing.

London's "strength of utterance" is at its height in his stories, and they are painstakingly well-constructed. "To Build a Fire" is the best known of all his stories. Set in the harsh Klondike, it recounts the haphazard trek of a new arrival who has ignored an old-timer's warning about the risks of traveling alone. Falling through the ice into a creek in seventy-five-below weather, the unnamed man is keenly aware that survival depends on his untested skills at quickly building a fire to dry his clothes and warm his extremities. After publishing a tame version of this story—with a sunny outcome—in The Youth's Companion in 1902, London offered a second, more severe take on the man's predicament in The Century Magazine in 1908. Reading both provides an illustration of London's growth and maturation as a writer. As Labor (1994) observes: "To compare the two versions is itself an instructive lesson in what distinguished a great work of literary art from a good children's story."

Other stories from the Klondike period include: "All Gold Canyon", about a battle between a gold prospector and a claim jumper; "The Law of Life", about an aging American Indian man abandoned by his tribe and left to die; "Love of Life", about a trek by a prospector across the Canadian tundra; "To the Man on Trail," which tells the story of a prospector fleeing the Mounted Police in a sled race, and raises the question of the contrast between written law and morality; and "An Odyssey of the North," which raises questions of conditional morality, and paints a sympathetic portrait of a man of mixed White and Aleut ancestry.

London was a boxing fan and an avid amateur boxer. "A Piece of Steak" is a tale about a match between older and younger boxers. It contrasts the differing experiences of youth and age but also raises the social question of the treatment of aging workers. "The Mexican" combines boxing with a social theme, as a young Mexican endures an unfair fight and ethnic prejudice to earn money with which to aid the revolution.

Several of London's stories would today be classified as science fiction. "The Unparalleled Invasion" describes germ warfare against China; "Goliath" is about an irresistible energy weapon; "The Shadow and the Flash" is a tale about two brothers who take different routes to achieving invisibility; "A

Relic of the Pliocene" is a tall tale about an encounter of a modern-day man with a mammoth. "The Red One" is a late story from a period when London was intrigued by the theories of the psychiatrist and writer Jung. It tells of an island tribe held in thrall by an extraterrestrial object.

Some nineteen original collections of short stories were published during London's brief life or shortly after his death. There have been several posthumous anthologies drawn from this pool of stories. Many of these stories were located in the Klondike and the Pacific. A collection of Jack London's San Francisco Stories was published in October 2010 by Sydney Samizdat Press.

Novels

London's most famous novels are The Call of the Wild, White Fang, The Sea-Wolf, The Iron Heel, and Martin Eden.

In a letter dated December 27, 1901, London's Macmillan publisher George Platt Brett, Sr., said "he believed Jack's fiction represented 'the very best kind of work' done in America."

Critic Maxwell Geismar called The Call of the Wild "a beautiful prose poem"; editor Franklin Walker said that it "belongs on a shelf with Walden and Huckleberry Finn"; and novelist E.L. Doctorow called it "a mordant parable ... his masterpiece."

The historian Dale L. Walker commented:

Jack London was an uncomfortable novelist, that form too long for his natural impatience and the quickness of his mind. His novels, even the best of them, are hugely flawed.

Some critics have said that his novels are episodic and resemble linked short stories. Dale L. Walker writes:

The Star Rover, that magnificent experiment, is actually a series of short stories connected by a unifying device ... Smoke Bellew is a series of stories bound together in a novel-like form by their reappearing protagonist, Kit Bellew; and John Barleycorn ... is a synoptic series of short episodes.

Ambrose Bierce said of The Sea-Wolf that "the great thing—and it is among the greatest of things—is that tremendous creation, Wolf Larsen ... the hewing out and setting up of such a figure is enough for a man to do in one lifetime. "However, he noted, "The love element, with its absurd suppressions, and impossible proprieties, is awful."

The Iron Heel is an example of a dystopian novel that anticipates and influenced George Orwell's Nineteen Eighty-Four. London's socialist politics are explicitly on display here. The Iron Heel meets the contemporary definition of soft science fiction. The Star Rover (1915) is also science fiction.

Apocrypha

Jack London Credo

London's literary executor, Irving Shepard, quoted a Jack London Credo in an introduction to a 1956 collection of London stories:

> I would rather be ashes than dust!
>
> I would rather that my spark should burn out in a brilliant blaze than it should be stifled by dry-rot.
>
> I would rather be a superb meteor, every atom of me in magnificent glow, than a sleepy and permanent planet.
>
> The function of man is to live, not to exist.
>
> I shall not waste my days in trying to prolong them.
>
> I shall use my time.

The biographer Stasz notes that the passage "has many marks of London's style" but the only line that could be safely attributed to London was the first. The words Shepard quoted were from a story in the San Francisco Bulletin, December 2, 1916, by journalist Ernest J. Hopkins, who visited the ranch just weeks before London's death. Stasz notes, "Even more so than today journalists' quotes were unreliable or even sheer inventions," and says no direct source in London's writings has been found. However, at least one line, according to Stasz, is authentic, being referenced by London and written in his own hand in the autograph book of Australian suffragette Vida Goldstein:

Dear Miss Goldstein:–

Seven years ago I wrote you that I'd rather be ashes than dust. I still subscribe to that sentiment.

Sincerely yours,

Jack London

Jan. 13, 1909

In his short story "By The Turtles of Tasman", a character, defending her "ne'er-do-well grasshopperish father" to her "antlike uncle", says: "... my father has been a king. He has lived .... Have you lived merely to live? Are you afraid to die? I'd rather sing one wild song and burst my heart with it, than live a thousand years watching my digestion and being afraid of the wet. When you are dust, my father will be ashes."

"The Scab"

A short diatribe on "The Scab" is often quoted within the U.S. labor movement and frequently attributed to London. It opens:

After God had finished the rattlesnake, the toad, and the vampire, he had some awful substance left with which he made a scab. A scab is a two-legged animal with a corkscrew soul, a water brain, a combination backbone of jelly and glue. Where others have hearts, he carries a tumor of rotten principles. When a scab comes down the street, men turn their backs and Angels weep in Heaven, and the Devil shuts the gates of hell to keep him out....

In 1913 and 1914, a number of newspapers printed the first three sentences with varying terms used instead of "scab", such as "knocker", "stool pigeon" or "scandal monger"

This passage as given above was the subject of a 1974 Supreme Court case, Letter Carriers v. Austin, in which Justice Thurgood Marshall referred to it as "a well-known piece of trade union literature, generally attributed to author Jack London". A union newsletter had published a "list of scabs," which was granted to be factual and therefore not libelous, but then went on to quote the passage as the "definition of a scab". The case turned on the question of whether the "definition" was defamatory. The court ruled that "Jack London's... 'definition of a scab' is merely rhetorical hyperbole, a lusty and imaginative expression of the contempt felt by union members towards those who refuse to join", and as such was not libelous and was protected under the First Amendment.

Despite being frequently attributed to London, the passage does not appear at all in the extensive collection of his writings at Sonoma State University's website. However, in his book The War of the Classes he published a 1903 speech entitled "The Scab", which gave a much more balanced view of the topic:

> The laborer who gives more time or strength or skill for the same wage than another, or equal time or strength or skill for a less wage, is a scab. The generousness on his part is hurtful to his fellow-laborers, for it compels them to an equal generousness which is not to their liking, and which gives them less of food and shelter. But a word may be said for the scab. Just as his act makes his rivals compulsorily generous, so do they, by fortune of birth and training, make compulsory his act of generousness.

> [...]

> Nobody desires to scab, to give most for least. The ambition of every individual is quite the opposite, to give least for most; and, as a result, living in a tooth-and-nail society, battle royal is waged by the ambitious individuals. But in its most salient aspect, that of the struggle over the division of the joint product, it is no longer a battle between individuals, but between groups of individuals. Capital and labor apply

themselves to raw material, make something useful out of it, add to its value, and then proceed to quarrel over the division of the added value. Neither cares to give most for least. Each is intent on giving less than the other and on receiving more.

Legacy and honors

Mount London, also known as Boundary Peak 100, on the Alaska-British Columbia boundary, in the Boundary Ranges of the Coast Mountains of British Columbia, is named for him.

Jack London Square on the waterfront of Oakland, California was named for him.

He was honored by the United States Postal Service with a 25¢ Great Americans series postage stamp released on January 11, 1986.

Jack London Lake (Russian), a mountain lake located in the upper reaches of the Kolyma River in Yagodninsky district of Magadan Oblast.

Fictional portrayals of London include Michael O'Shea in the 1943 film Jack London, Jeff East in the 1980 film Klondike Fever, Aaron Ashmore in the Murdoch Mysteries episode "Murdoch of the Klondike" from 2012, and Johnny Simmons in the 2014 miniseries Klondike. (Source: Wikipedia)

NOTABLE WORKS

NOVELS

The Cruise of the Dazzler (1902)

A Daughter of the Snows (1902)

The Call of the Wild (1903)

The Kempton-Wace Letters (1903) (published anonymously, co-authored with Anna Strunsky)

The Sea-Wolf (1904)

The Game (1905)

White Fang (1906)

Before Adam (1907)

The Iron Heel (1908)

Martin Eden (1909)

Burning Daylight (1910)

Adventure (1911)

The Scarlet Plague (1912)

A Son of the Sun (1912)

The Abysmal Brute (1913)

The Valley of the Moon (1913)

The Mutiny of the Elsinore (1914)

The Star Rover (1915) (published in England as The Jacket)

The Little Lady of the Big House (1916)

Jerry of the Islands (1917)

Michael, Brother of Jerry (1917)

Hearts of Three (1920) (novelization of a script by Charles Goddard)

The Assassination Bureau, Ltd (1963) (left half-finished, completed by Robert L. Fish)

SHORT STORIES

"An Old Soldier's Story" (1894)

"Who Believes in Ghosts!" (1895)

"And 'FRISCO Kid Came Back" (1895)

"Night's Swim In Yeddo Bay" (1895)

"One More Unfortunate" (1895)

"Sakaicho, Hona Asi And Hakadaki" (1895)

"A Klondike Christmas" (1897)

"Mahatma's Little Joke" (1897)

"O Haru" (1897)

"Plague Ship" (1897)

"The Strange Experience Of A Misogynist" (1897)

"Two Gold Bricks" (1897)

"The Devil's Dice Box" (1898)

"A Dream Image" (1898)

"The Test: A Clondyke Wooing" (1898)

"To the Man on Trail" (1898)

"In a Far Country" (1899)

"The King of Mazy May" (1899)

"The End Of The Chapter" (1899)

"The Grilling Of Loren Ellery" (1899)

"The Handsome Cabin Boy" (1899)

"In The Time Of Prince Charley" (1899)

"Old Baldy" (1899)

"The Men of Forty Mile" (1899)

"Pluck and Pertinacity" (1899)

"The Rejuvenation of Major Rathbone" (1899)

"The White Silence" (1899)

"A Thousand Deaths" (1899)

"Wisdom of the Trail" (1899)

"An Odyssey of the North" (1900)

"The Son of the Wolf" (1900)

"Even unto Death" (1900)

"The Man with the Gash" (1900)

"A Lesson in Heraldry" (1900)

"A Northland Miracle" (1900)

"Proper "GIRLIE"" (1900)

"Thanksgiving on Slav Creek" (1900)

"Their Alcove" (1900)

"Housekeeping in the Klondike" (1900)

"Dutch Courage" (1900)

"Where the Trail Forks" (1900)

"Hyperborean Brew" (1901)

"A Relic of the Pliocene" (1901)

"The Lost Poacher" (1901)

"The God of His Fathers" (1901)

""FRISCO Kid's" Story" (1901)

"The Law of Life" (1901)

"The Minions of Midas" (1901)

"In the Forests of the North" (1902)

"The "Fuzziness" of Hoockla-Heen" (1902)

"The Story of Keesh" (1902)

"Keesh, Son of Keesh" (1902)

"Nam-Bok, the Unveracious" (1902)

"Li Wan the Fair" (1902)

"Lost Face"

"Master of Mystery" (1902)

"The Sunlanders" (1902)

"The Death of Ligoun" (1902)

"Moon-Face" (1902)

"Diable—A Dog" (1902), renamed Bâtard in 1904

"To Build a Fire" (1902, revised 1908)

"The League of the Old Men" (1902)

"The Dominant Primordial Beast" (1903)

"The One Thousand Dozen" (1903)

"The Marriage of Lit-lit" (1903)

"The Shadow and the Flash" (1903)

"The Leopard Man's Story" (1903)

"Negore the Coward" (1904)

"All Gold Cañon" (1905)

"Love of Life" (1905)

"The Sun-Dog Trail" (1905)

"The Apostate" (1906)

"Up the Slide" (1906)

"Planchette" (1906)

"Brown Wolf" (1906)

"Make Westing" (1907)

"Chased by the Trail" (1907)

"Trust" (1908)

"A Curious Fragment" (1908)

"Aloha Oe" (1908)

"That Spot" (1908)

"The Enemy of All the World" (1908)

"The House of Mapuhi" (1909)

"Good-by, Jack" (1909)

"Samuel" (1909)

"South of the Slot" (1909)

"The Chinago" (1909)

"The Dream of Debs" (1909)

"The Madness of John Harned" (1909)

"The Seed of McCoy" (1909)

"A Piece of Steak" (1909)

"Mauki" (1909)

"The Whale Tooth" (1909)

"Goliath" (1910)

"The Unparalleled Invasion" (1910)

"Told in the Drooling Ward" (1910)

"When the World was Young" (1910)

"The Terrible Solomons" (1910)

"The Inevitable White Man" (1910)

"The Heathen" (1910)

"Yah! Yah! Yah!" (1910)

"By the Turtles of Tasman" (1911)

"The Mexican" (1911)

"War" (1911)

"The Unmasking of the Cad" (1911)

"The Scarlet Plague" (1912)

"The Captain of the Susan Drew" (1912)

"The Sea-Farmer" (1912)

"The Feathers of the Sun" (1912)

"The Prodigal Father" (1912)

"Samuel" (1913)

"The Sea-Gangsters" (1913)

"The Strength of the Strong" (1914)

"Told in the Drooling Ward" (1914)

"The Hussy" (1916)

"Like Argus of the Ancient Times" (1917)

"Jerry of the Islands" (1917)

"The Red One" (1918)

"Shin-Bones" (1918)

"The Bones of Kahekili" (1919)

SHORT STORY COLLECTIONS

Son of the Wolf (1900)

Chris Farrington, Able Seaman (1901)

The God of His Fathers & Other Stories (1901)

Children of the Frost (1902)

The Faith of Men and Other Stories (1904)

Tales of the Fish Patrol (1906)

Moon-Face and Other Stories (1906)

Love of Life and Other Stories (1907)

Lost Face (1910)

South Sea Tales (1911)

When God Laughs and Other Stories (1911)

The House of Pride & Other Tales of Hawaii (1912)

Smoke Bellew (1912)

A Son of the Sun (1912)

The Night Born (1913)

The Strength of the Strong (1914)

The Turtles of Tasman (1916)

The Human Drift (1917)

The Red One (1918)

On the Makaloa Mat (1919)

Dutch Courage and Other Stories (1922)

AUTOBIOGRAPHICAL MEMOIRS

The Road (1907)

The Cruise of the Snark (1911)

John Barleycorn (1913)

NON-FICTION AND ESSAYS

Through the Rapids on the Way to the Klondike (1899)

From Dawson to the Sea (1899)

What Communities Lose by the Competitive System (1900)

The Impossibility of War (1900)

Phenomena of Literary Evolution (1900)

A Letter to Houghton Mifflin Co. (1900)

Husky, Wolf Dog of the North (1900)

Editorial Crimes — A Protest (1901)

Again the Literary Aspirant (1902)

The People of the Abyss (1903)

How I Became a Socialist (1903)

The War of the Classes (1905)

The Story of an Eyewitness (1906)

A Letter to Woman's Home Companion (1906)

Revolution, and other Essays (1910)

Mexico's Army and Ours (1914)

Lawgivers (1914)

Our Adventures in Tampico (1914)

Stalking the Pestilence (1914)

The Red Game of War (1914)

The Trouble Makers of Mexico (1914)

With Funston's Men (1914)

POETRY

A Heart (1899)

Abalone Song (1913)

And Some Night (1914)

Ballade of the False Lover (1914)

Cupid's Deal (1913)

Daybreak (1901)

Effusion (1901)

George Sterling (1913)

Gold (1915)

He Chortled with Glee (1899)

He Never Tried Again (1912)

His Trip to Hades (1913)

Homeland (1914)

Hors de Saison (1913)

If I Were God (1899)

In a Year (1901)

In and Out (1911)

Je Vis en Espoir (1897)

Memory (1913)

Moods (1913)

My Confession (1912)

My Little Palmist (1914)

Of Man of the Future (1915)

Oh You Everybody's Girl (19)

On the Face of the Earth You are the One (1915)

Rainbows End (1914)

Republican Rallying Song (1916)

Sonnet (1901)

The Gift of God (1905)

The Klondyker's Dream (1914)

The Lover's Liturgy (1913)

The Mammon Worshippers (1911)

The Republican Battle-Hymn (1905)

The Return of Ulysses (1915)

The Sea Sprite and the Shooting Star (1916)

The Socialist's Dream (1912)

The Song of the Flames (1903)

The Way of War (1906)

The Worker and the Tramp (1911)

Tick! Tick! Tick! (1915)

Too Late (1912)

Weasel Thieves (1913)

When All the World Shouted my Name (1905)

Where the Rainbow Fell (1902)

Your Kiss (1914)

PLAYS

Theft (1910)

Daughters of the Rich: A One Act Play (1915)

The Acorn Planter: A California Forest Play (1916)

CPSIA information can be obtained
at www.ICGtesting.com
Printed in the USA
LVHW020235150920
665985LV00001B/130

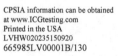

9 789390 262922